Seaweed Pirates

By

Joey Gnarly

Gnarlyfest Publications

Copyright 2021 © Joey Gnarly

An Imprint of Gnarlyfest

All rights reserved.

Printed in the United States of America.

No part of this book may be used or reproduced in any manner whatsoever without written permission except in the case of true quotations embodied in critical articles and reviews.

For information address: Gnarlyfest online.

Library of Congress Cataloging in Publication Data

Gnarlyfest

ISBN 9798712790975

Published by Gnarlyfest

Seaweed Pirates

By

Joey Gnarly

Day 1

Like Christmas morning, it had come without warning, an amazingly magical day for stoners around the world. It was 4/20 and we were high; shit, we were higher than high. We were stoney bologny. Sun rays highlighted by smoke trails and waves of clouds wafted through the foggy room that smelled something like the inside of a nugget. When just then, Booger walked in. Booger was a strait-laced dude, kinda serious, with bursts of laughter… actually, he might legit be bipolar, very up and down.

"Where'd you get that?" I asked right away. I thought it was so strange, like did he take it from school or something?

He was holding a whiteboard in his hands.

"Found it in someone's trash on the way over," he replied while making a suspiciously curious face as if we were ignoring the fact that my place was fish-bowled.

"What's going on?" he slowly questioned us, "Did someone win the Lotto or whose B-day is it?"

He was just getting back from summer school and we all met every day at my shed to smoke and chill and jam.

"It's 4/20, man," Dave exclaimed and then asked, "You forgot?!"

"No, it's just not that big a deal," Booger said, but clearly he forgot and just didn't want to admit it.

"Not that big a deal?" I said. "Not that big a deal? It's our only holiday!" I added.

"We smoke every day. What's the difference?" Booger asked.

"Well, we eat every day, too, but there's only one Thanksgiving," I answered, and with that I grabbed the whiteboard.

"Let me see this, who wants to go on an adventure?" I asked.

"What kind of adventure?" asked Dave.

"The search for Sensemilla Island," I said in a pirate voice.

"Haha, yes!" coughed Sean, smoke shooting out of his mouth.

"Shut up," said Booger.

"Down," said Dave.

"First of all, it doesn't exist. And second of all, how would we travel? We only have my car and I'm not risking it on a journey. I need it for school and work," Booger said as if that was the end of it.

"First of all, bro, it does exist and if not, it would be a fun thing to do, or we can just keep doing nothing. Second of all, we can buy a van together, or better yet, let's get a boat!" I said as Sean and Dave cheered and took fat rips.

I had heard of this legend of the Sensemilla Island almost as a diss from a preppy dude at some sailing class I tried once, but clearly didn't fit in.

"What, you here to learn to sail so you can find Sensemilla Island?" scoffed the preppy d-bag.

I later researched to see if this place was real and it kind of was. The myth is that there's a certain area where drug smugglers have to get through as they travel by boat, bringing the drugs from their country. Many times they just throw it overboard and into the water which will later wash up on land, or sometimes you can find them floating in the ocean. These are called square groupers.

There is a little island close to the coast of Key West that is a hot spot of smuggling activity and there you will find Sensemilla Island where pounds of weed wash up daily and you can smoke happily ever after.

The week before I had been held at gunpoint while delivering pizza, so I wasn't kidding. It was the summer after school and I was looking for a new beginning. That's just not the way I wanna go, ya know? Maybe riding a big wave in Hawaii or sky diving from space, but not delivering pizza.

It ended up a joke anyway, the guy said, "Ha ha just kidding," and handed me a blunt and a shot of vodka and back to work I went, life still flashing before my eyes along with horrific images of the shotgun barrel in my face lit by the trailer's porch light. They knew I was serious, too.

I said, "C'mon guys! By land or by sea?" as I hung the drawing board on the wall and started writing the pros and cons of traveling by land in a van or by sea in a boat.

Van	Boat
<u>Free</u> Parking lot camping	<u>Free</u> to anchor
No bathroom	Bathroom <u>all around</u> <u>Free</u>
Gas $$$	Wind <u>Free</u>
Roads/Accidents	Open waters smooth sailing
	Myth of Square Groupers

It was all becoming very clear, very quick, or so we thought...

Booger thought it was all a joke, but for me, Sean, and Dave it was the answer.

"So we all agree? Sailboat is the way to go?!" I asked like a rhetorical question.

"Pshh what?! No!" Booger retorted.

"What do you mean, Boog?" I asked even though I already knew he was never coming with us.

"This isn't real life. You guys aren't thinking this through," he blasted omnisciently.

"What's there to think about? I say we make a choice here and now on this crusty shell-patterned couch. Will we live the lives they want us to live? Or will we blaze our own trails and set sail? Let's at least give it a shot before we can only wish we had. We can always come back and get a real job and start again."

At this point I felt like I was preaching. It was true but funny in a surreal, life changing moment kind of way. Up until now, Sean and Dave had just been quietly passing the bong 'til they both said, "I'm down," and looked at each other and laughed.

"Yeah we'll be called the Seaweed Pirates 'cause when we see weed, we smoke it!" Sean shouted and laughed, Booger sat down and started packing a bowl.

I looked up local boat listings, found a few of the cheapest sailboats for sail and checked the Internet reviews for each one. The review for the cheapest, closest one claimed it was unsinkable, easy choice.

"You guys wanna go check it out?" I asked.

"Word," said Dave.

"Sure," said Sean.

"Meh," Booger sighed.

"Nice, let's go!" I said and then called the owner of the boat to tell him we were interested and asked if we could look at it now. He sounded excited and so were we.

On the way we got lost and it was starting to get dark by the time we got there. We pulled up to a nice house on the Intercoastal and were greeted by a man who was rather shocked at our strange crew.

"Do any of you have any prior sailing experience at all?" he asked while looking like he smelled something foul. Maybe he did, maybe he smelled all the weed on us… oops. It was then I realized we were like beach bums at a yacht club.

"Yes," I spoke up after an awkward moment, "I took a sailing class once."

"Oh alright," he said quickly as he led us to the backyard and onto the deck of the boat.

There it was. A beautiful white, green, and wooden sailboat. It had a cabin that could sleep three comfortably and a bathroom and kitchen area! There was bench like seats/beds covered in green fabric, everything trimmed with old beautiful wood. It was a lot to take in and none of us had ever inspected a boat or even really been on sailboats ever. Let alone make sure it's ready for a voyage, but we all thought it looked pretty cool.

I looked at the boys, they nodded, and, "We'll take it," I said.

"Perfect, I'll need it gone by the morning," he said as he took the money and put it into his breast pocket.

We looked at each other stuttering and staring. We had thought we could buy it and come back and pick it up later. We were not ready to start the journey, we had not packed anything, no clothes, no food, and no weed!

He told us if we couldn't get it out of there, the deal was off, and someone else would be taking it tomorrow. I knew what I needed to do.

"There's a nice marina around the corner," he said.

"Awesome. Can you take me there?"

"Take you?" the seller replied.

"Yeah. It's been a while, it would be so great if you could go with me on the boat."

"I guess I could do that. I'll have my wife pick me up there at the marina."

He seemed a bit uncomfortable, but so were we, everything from here on out was new and unexpected. I felt a pull at my shirt.

"Can we talk real quick?" Booger said as he pulled me into a group huddle with Sean and Dave.

"What are we doing?" asked Dave.

"Yeah, is this gonna work?" Sean chimed in.

"I got this," I said as I tried to make it all work.

"I'll go, I'll go to the marina on the boat, and meet you guys there."

"And then what?!" snapped Booger.

"And then we either spend the night there or anchor in the Bay," I said.

"We're not ready for any of this," Booger said.

At this point, Sean and Dave didn't look too sure or too high, the weed was wearing off and 4/20 was coming to an end. Things were becoming too real. It went from a fun idea on a high day to life-changing situations that we didn't understand.

"Let's just go with the flow, worse comes to worst you can walk away," I said to the guys as I started towards Mr. Hoffendoer, I finally learned his name as I read it on the receipt he handed me and we got into the boat.

"See you guys there!" I yelled back as we set off slowly down the dark canal lit only by the dock lights of mansions and their giant windows. It was late now and we were alone, silently cruising on the water, slowly, as thoughts raced through my mind. What *do* I do now? This is our boat? So crazy, I'm a boat owner haha. We weren't sailing, the boat also had a little motor which I thought was great!

"Would you like some sausage?" Hoffendoer asked quaintly as he handed me a delicious smelling Italian sausage in a sandwich baggie. It must have been obvious how caught off guard I was because he went on to explain his wife had made them for dinner but the deal had interrupted so she thought we might want some on the ride.

"Yes, please!"

I was starving, or at least had the munchies like crazy. It was delicious and brought energy back to my brain.

"Thank you so much, oh wow, this is delicious… Okay so this is the engine? Just regular gas?" I started realizing I better take note of how to run this vessel, "How do you work the sails?" I asked.

"I thought you knew how to do this?" he replied.

"It's just been a while," I said.

"Oh, well, I'll come back in the morning and show you," he said as we pulled into the marina.

Oh shit we're here, I thought to myself, realizing I honestly had no idea what to do or what would come next. Thankfully, the boys were there waiting for me. It was reassuring that I wasn't alone in this.

"Aye!" Dave yelled cheerfully as Sean at the same time shouted, "Hey hey!"

And Booger was just kinda mumbling something probably negative as he kicked rocks.

I couldn't blame him though really, it *was* getting late and I may have bit off more than we could chew plus I think he had summer school in the morning.

"Dudes, she's a beauty!" I said as we all met up and exchanged a mixture of daps and high-fives.

"Thank you so much, man!" I yelled at Hoffendoer.

"Thank you," the boys all added in as Hoffendoer climbed into his SUV and shouted back in a tired yet optimistic sounding voice, "You're welcome, see you tomorrow!" as he and his wife pulled out of the rocky parking lot. You could hear the rocks crushing under the tires in the night as it drove off.

It was a very nice looking marina, I hadn't been to many but I have driven by enough to know this one looked fancy, which had me a little worried because this could mean it was expensive to be here. It was too late for any of that to matter, the boat was docked and it was no longer the boat, it was our boat.

"So what now?" Dave asked as we stood in an eerily empty and strangely silent parking lot, completely sober by now.

"Now we go home," Booger said sternly, "I've got shit to do tomorrow," he added.

"Same," said Sean begrudgingly.

You know that shitty feeling you get when you go over a weird little hill too fast in a car? It's like your stomach falling out of your ass, it was that feeling times ten as I stared at them jaw dropped trying to find the words to say. Then like synchronized swimmers with perfectly choreographed timing, they each made a move for the doors of Booger's car.

"You got this bro!" Sean said as he sat down into the car.

Before I could say much, it seemed like they were already driving away. Like I said, I can't blame them, it was my crazy idea and they had some things they had to clear up. We agreed they'd be back the next day with supplies.

As I made my way back to the boat by myself, I couldn't help but take notice once again at how fancy this place was. The path back to the boat dock was large, white, concrete squares with shell-like patterns engraved in each, and surrounded by small stone or crushed shell. The path was so clean as if it was pressure washed every day and lit by these little glowing landscaping path lights. There was even a gate with a key code box on it to get down to the actual dock where the boat was tied up. Thankfully, that was unlocked and open when we got here. For a moment I was worried I wouldn't recognize my sailboat from the others like when you forget where you parked your car, but nope, there she was, sticking out like a sore thumb. She was beautiful, but she was much different than the surrounding ships. They were newer but not better, they looked more plastic and shiny. Mine had an older wooden vibe, I mentioned before the trimming of grainy wood lined along the edges of everything. The pine green matching fabrics from our sail cover to the bench seats had a Gatsby kind of vibe and all around she had personality. I walked over to her slowly, like I was approaching an untamed animal, looked at her up and down and jumped in.

"Ttthhh, Aaahhh," I took a deep breath in and let it out, with my arms outstretched just taking it all in. This was my boat? It still didn't feel real. I stepped up onto the roof of the cabin and took a seat. I sat and stared at the sky wondering what I had just done that day, then I started thinking what I was going to do the next day. I know these marinas cost money and I really had none left at all. My plans went as far as get boat, find Sensemilla Island, live like a pirate. Beyond that I thought we'd just figure it out.

I went down into the cabin and laid on a bench. There were three, one was at the front of the boat and was triangle shaped to fit in the front of the boat, and there was a bench on either side of the cabin. One was short and the other was full-length, but from the knees down your legs went into a creepy coffin like place. I chose the shorter side bench. I was just dozing off when a chattering, clicking noise started almost faintly in the distance. It went on clicking, tapping, crackling, it was like that cereal Crispy Pops or something. My mind started creating possibilities of what this unknown sound could be. Rats? Mice? Bugs of sorts? Is the boat falling apart? Is that the sound of water leaking in every crevice? Will I wake up on a sunken boat? I had thought myself into a slumber, and like that it was over.

Day 2

The sun was rising, I had made it through the night! I stood stretched and let out a grunt, "Wooo!" I thought to myself and obviously out loud.

"Hello?" a voice came from outside on the dock.

Oh shit oh shit oh shit, was I in trouble? Am I supposed to be here? What do I say? Should I stay quiet? No, I just said, Woo like a freaking rodeo clown, "Uh, ha ha, hey," I laughed and greeted the man as I poked my head out.

"Where'd you come from?" he replied shortly and that wasn't meant to be a joke about his height, but he was a short little dude with a whistle.

I was thinking, should I reply my life story and heritage to try to get a quick laugh and break the ice, or was this one of those more serious moments? It was all starting to feel like a delusional dream.

"Bought this boat around the corner last night. Owner needed it gone. And this is my first boat and I wasn't sure what to do," I said.

"Well, it's $80 a night to dock here," he cut me off.

"Okay, cool, I don't have any cash on me now, but my friends will be here today!" I barely finished the words and he was on his way back to the main office building.

I turned and looked back at our sailboat, I was seeing her for the first time in daylight. She was dirty, but boy was she purty, I laughed to myself. Which reminded me, where were my friends?

Just then, another dude with the same color shirt and shorts as the last dude but no whistle, came right up to me and said, "You just bought this boat?"

"Yep," I now replied shortly as I was feeling a little overwhelmed.

"How much?" he asked instantly.

"I'd rather not say," I replied again, I was feeling bombarded and needed to get a hold of my friends.

"That's cool, great boat, man. Can I come aboard, check her out?" he asked, "I'm Tod."

I could see his nametag TODD. He seemed like a nice guy, little quirky, but nice.

"Yeah man, come on in," I said.

We started talking and it turns out he is a fellow stoner, so we hit it off right away. He wanted to know the whole story of how and why I have this boat, so I told him and by some cosmic coincidence, Todd tells me he's got the same goal to someday leave on his sailboat and find the legendary Sensemilla Island.

Well, at that point I already knew this was one of those interactions that was just meant to be.

"Oops, my breaks up ten minutes ago," he said as he bounced out the cabin door and off the boat, "I'll be back when my shift ends at 9:00 pm."

"K, cool," I shouted, "Thank you," I shouted again.

He told me that when the first little guy with the whistle went back inside he was basically talking trash and it piqued Tod's interest. Todd also told me I might be able to get that night for free and not have to pay the $80. But I won't know till 9:00 pm, which is when the boat needs to be gone from the marina by or technically it's another night I will owe. I finally decide it's time to hit up the boys and sent them a text.

Me: [What's good?]

Dave: [NM U?]

… Excuse me what? wait hold on, I'm thinking, he didn't really just say that. It meant, "Nothing much, how about you."

Me: [Dude I'm on a ducking boat! Waiting for y'all]

Dave: [You're on a duck boat?]

I was trying to remain calm while having very nearly a meltdown of some kind.

Sean: [No dude he's on our boat]

Dave: [Wow! I thought that was a dream]

Booger: [I was hoping it was a nightmare]

Me: [Please come soon]

Me: [with weed]

As I was approaching my peak of overwhelmedness a voice called out like a Reggae angel, "Aye, Ras!"

"Aye, Ras!" the man repeated.

I didn't know who it was but I knew they were talking to me.

I had dreads at the time, long thick, wild Marley style locks and Ras meant Rasta, it is a title for men practicing Rastafarian culture. I didn't think of myself as Rasta, but when I was in Jamaica one time hanging out with the real Rastafarians they told me besides the lifestyle, Rasta was in the heart and that I was a true Rasta at heart.

I looked over to see where the voice was coming from. There behind the locked gate a man also with dreads ... gripping the black chain link with both hands, his face pressed against the fencing as if to attempt to get closer.

I stood on the bow and waved back.

"Yooo!" he started gesturing for me to come over and then said, "Bro, come here."

Life was hitting me faster than usual with the choices to make and it was starting to feel like it was becoming a new reoccurring theme. I wanted to say hi, but I felt like I was already in trouble with the marina. What if this guy was trouble? I don't know anymore, I thought to myself. I'm getting tired of thinking. I jumped off onto the dock and ran up to the fence.

"What's good, brudda?! Do I know you?"

Maybe we had met before at a concert?

"Na fam, I just see a dready on a boat and had to holler," he replied.

"Oh word," I nodded.

"Is that your boat?" he asked.

"Yeah, man! Just got her," I said.

"No way! That's so awesome. Can I check it out?" he asked. He could tell I wasn't 100 percent sure, he went on, "It's no worries," like if I didn't want him to come check it out.

"Yeah, no, for sure, man, I just don't know the rules of this place and shit, but yeah, come on down," I said.

He had dreads and a guitar on his back, he was already practically family. We made our way to the boat as I told him how I had just gotten it last night and how I was kind of in limbo with my friends and the whole deal with the dock.

He was really impressed by the boat and told me he had a sailboat and it was at another marina somewhere and he travelled back and forth between this one and that, I guess, I don't know, but he knew stuff about sailboats, so I believed him.

He started pointing out things that were and were not working, a big one seemed to be the center board. It was jammed and he told me without that there wasn't much real sailing to be done. When I heard that, I about shit my pants but he said it could be an easy fix if the line that controlled it wasn't damaged.

"Might just be barnacled up, bro," he said, as he could see the enthusiasm draining from my face.

"Names Ty by the way," he said, I think trying to break the silence.

"Oh my bad man, names Joe, I'm so out of it," I said.

"Ha ha," we both laughed.

"Hey you wanna jam?" I asked.

"Yeah man, what you got?" he asked, like what will I jam on, what instrument.

I reached for a little bucket that had some nails and knick knacks in it and dumped it on the counter, flipped it over and held it upside down between my knees.

"I'll tap on this plus I'm usually the vocals for the bands I'm in," I said.

"What, no way, me too man," he said, "Let's do it den," he yelled as he opened his guitar. "Freestyle or cover?" Ty asked.

"Freestyle," I replied and for the next hour or so we jammed and created a song that was something different, something amazing, and something straight from the heart.

It was meditation at its finest.

He strummed and I drummed and we both added verses made up on the spot that cohesively unified to make verbal art, at least that's how we felt.

"Whoa, whoa, whoa! Hello!" whistle man yelled over the sounds we were making.

"Yes, hi," I said.

"You can't do that here," the man said.

"K sorry, I'm waiting for Tod," I said.

He walked off.

"Sorry man, didn't mean to cause a stir," Ty said as he started packing up.

"Na, no stress man. Was great meeting you!" I said.

"Brudda, I'm in a band that's always touring and gigging. You are welcome on stage with us anytime," Ty said.

I was honored to say the least. We did one of those one armed guy hugs and he was gone.

The last fifteen hours or so of my life had been fleeting and maybe a little dare I say crazy but I had done plenty of crazy shit in life, I was that dude down for anything that led to a good time. Don't get me wrong though, I always did my research first and made sure I knew a little about something before I dove in. It was 5 o'clock and time suddenly came to a halt. There was still four hours before Todd got off work and I still needed to know if I had to pay for last night and would I stay again this night or anchor nearby for free? Plus where the hell were my…

"Yo!"

"Hey!"

"Oh!"

"Aye!"

A crowd cheering? Maybe some people watching sports on tv at the marina bar? I was just going to lay in our boat in the triangle part at the front, it was great because it had a hatch that opened up to the top deck, it was heavy and solid with tinted plexi-glass to let light in. Perfect spot to rest, but as I went to lay down the cheering roared again and was louder this time. I needed to see what was going on. I stood in the cabin and opened the hatch.

Bam!

It slammed back on the boat.

"Okay, gotta do that more gently next time," I said to myself as I popped out of the hole in the boat looking something like a prairie dog popping out of his ground home checking for danger.

And there in the glorious last golden rays of the day stood my friends and they were being approached by security…

"DUDES!" I shouted followed by, "They're with me! They're with me, sirs."

It was smiles all around. Even Booger had a smile on,

or he was squinting from the light, I'm not sure, but it felt great, and I could see they had my guitar, my djembe drum and a backpack of goodness. After that meeting with Ty, I texted the boys to bring the acoustic guitar and bongo drums, too. We were in an on again off again band that fluctuated with everyone's life schedules. Sometimes people would move away and then come back, some years in school were harder than others, it was just for fun. I was beyond glad to see them and the stuff they brought. We went right to our boat and they showed me everything they grabbed from my house for me, but I realized they didn't bring anything for them.

"Where's your stuff?" I questioned.

They looked at each other and I knew I would be alone again for at least another night.

"We aren't ready," Booger responded for the guys.

"Oh, okay, I see how it is," I said back.

"But hey bro bro, look what I brought you!" Sean said as he pulled out a bag of dank smelling bud from his pocket, about a gram.

"Yooo ho ho, yes brotha thank you! Thank you!" I exclaimed. It was as if the heavens opened up and angels sang.

"And here's some BK," Dave added.

"Oh my God yes, I love you guys, thank you."

"But no pipe," said Booger plainly.

Before anyone could utter another word, "You brought my guitar right?"

"Ha ha," we all laughed.

"Oh shit, I forgot," Sean said.

As a fun creative project for myself earlier that year I had added a little modification to my acoustic guitar. That's right, I turned my guitar into a pipe. Why not? I drilled two holes one for the bowl and one for the mouth piece and connected them with a rubber hose. I made it so I could smoke while jamming.

"What? I don't get it," Booger said.

"His guitar. It's a pipe, Bro," Dave said.

"Of course," said Booger.

"How was it?" Sean asked referring to the night I spent alone on the boat.

"It was good but we need to figure some shit out now," I replied not going into detail at all about the strange noises of the night.

"We might have to pay like $80 bucks for last night and $80 more for tonight unless we come up with another plan," I said.

"What happened to anchoring in the Bay?" Booger said.

"I've never anchored a boat at all, let alone by myself or in the night," I said as if I'd been thinking about it for a while.

"But you said," Booger started to say when I cut him off...

"I said I could sail, never said anything about knowing how to anchor."

Sean and Dave looked on wide-eyed then Dave added in, "We scrounged up $20 more."

I took the money silently and looked back at them as the three of them stared at me.

"Okay, no worries, it's all good," I said nodding my head with encouragement.

I knew then that I had gotten us into this and I needed to get us out.

"So you got this?" Sean asked sincerely.

"Yeah man you know I'll figure it out," I replied.

"Alright, well cool, we gotta go," Booger interjected.

I understood. They still needed to clear shit up and it was a little bit of a drive to get here, like forty minutes either way.

I appreciated the stuff but we hadn't figured anything out and they were gone as quick as they had come.

Time was different on a boat. I could tell and I hadn't even left the dock yet.

I laid down in the cabin for that much needed nap now since I must not have gotten much sleep the night before or was still tired from when,

Bang! Bang! Bang!

I shot up off the bench and got in a ready position, ready for what I don't know, ready for anything.

Bang! Bang! Bang!

Someone was legitimately smashing on my boat.

"Hey you in there?" a familiar voice shouted.

"Todd, dude," I yelled back emerging from the cabin. "I thought you were the cops or a bear, haha," I said laughing obviously happy to see him. He was smiling ear to ear and it was great to see and kind of funny because he was missing a tooth right in the front that seemed to add a lot of character. Todd was holding up a six pack of beer in one hand and a rolled up brown paper bag in the other.

"Nope not the cops man, it's just me," Todd said joyfully still smiling. "And I come bearing gifts," he added.

"Niiice," I said dragging it out to accentuate the awesomeness, "Welcome aboard," I added. I couldn't believe how late it had gotten, I must have slept a while, I thought to myself as we went down into the cabin. It was really dark in there.

"Do your lights work?" Todd asked.

"Oh I don't know, haven't tried," I said. "I don't even know where they would be haha," I said.

He laughed and said, "Uh I think these are them," he flicked a lighter to see what he was doing and flipped a switch on the wall.

"Yup, there ya go," he said as the lights in the cabin turned on.

"Wow would ya look at that!" I had no idea obviously because I had spent the night before in the dark. "Thanks man and thanks for coming back to hang," I said and meant it. It was nice to have anyone help at this point.

"You're welcome. And guess what?" Todd asked, "Got you last night free," he said proudly.

"My brudda! Thank you," I exclaimed as I jumped up rejuvenated with good news. "Dude, that's huge. I appreciate you so much!" I went on.

"No problem," Todd said as he started opening the brown paper bag and reaching for its mysterious contents. "Did you decide what you want to do tonight? Because I can't get you tonight free."

The joy in my face must have been slipping away because he quickly said, "Here want some hash?"

And like that I snapped back into the mood.

"Ha ha yes dude! I can't thank you enough! Can I just light it up here?" I asked.

It was an old wooden sherlock style tobacco pipe with a screen and a chunk of hash on it.

"Yeah," he said trying to assure me while looking unsure.

"Fuck it, awesome," I said and sparked the lighter simultaneously while going in for the hit, "Thank you, cheers," I said and took the first real hit in what seemed like days and it sure hit back.

"Caw hak kak caw," I coughed so hard.

"Ha ha ha ha," Todd blasted laughing.

"Hak hak hak, I joined in coughing and laughing, "Dude yes thank you," I continued thanking Todd. My eyes felt red and my face felt heavy. I was insta-high and in that moment it's all good, everything is all good.

"Wash it down with a brew?" Todd asked me.

"Nah, I don't really drink much," I replied feeling weird but it was the truth.

"Ah well, I got it for us and I came up with a plan if you want to try it out," Todd said.

"Thanks man, I can't even tell you how much I appreciate you and your help, definitely, lay it on me," I said.

"I know this is going to sound crazy but I have the same boat and the same dream as you and a dock across the bay you can stay at until you're ready for your journey," he said.

"What really!? That's amazing!" I exclaimed again. I didn't realize how amazing and how rare that really was. There were not many of these boats and the maker was a local legend. "That doesn't sound crazy, that sounds amazing," I said.

"Well, here's the crazy part, we need to sail it there tonight or you have to pay here," he said and went on to tell me how rare our boats were, it was more than a coincidence, but I couldn't help but start thinking of my other options. I started thinking, …Or I could anchor in the bay, what if this dude is crazy? Wait I don't know how to anchor, it's night time and I'd probably not be able to get a hold of my friends out there or anyone.

"Man this is getting crazy. Let me just call the other owners of the boat and see how they feel," I said.

"Yeah no problem," he replied.

"I'm gonna go lock up my truck and get stuff out I need in case we do go," he said.

"Word, I will make some calls real quick," I said.

And he went off the boat and up the dock ramp.

I called the boys. I called my mom. I told them both basically I don't know if this dude is psycho or for real, but it's our only option.

I say psycho because people just aren't that nice anymore in this world and sometimes you hear stories of crazy shit, you know what I mean.

But like I said, it was really the only option. Plus what are the odds, some dude named Todd has the same rare boat, same dream, and a free place to dock. It had to be written in the stars. And boy were they bright that night.

"What's the news?" Todd yelled as he emerged from the darkness down the dock.

"They said yes," I yelled back like they were the deciding factor when really I was just letting them know what I was doing and where I was going with Todd from the marina in case anything bad happened to me.

"Really?" he replied sounding like he didn't think it was really happening either.

"Yeah man let's do this!" I said enthusiastically.

"Alright," he said as he got a little more serious now knowing we were going, it was official.

"You got life jackets?" he asked as he started looking around assessing the situation at hand.

"Yup right here," I said and flipped open the bench seat to reveal a few old life jackets, salty and sun faded from years of use.

"Oh, nice," he said, but didn't look stoked."

"Gas in the tank?" he added as he went up and out of the cabin and checked the little outboard engine at the back of the boat.

"Oh shit, hopefully," I laughed and said but he looked more intense and serious like a different person now which I understood needed to happen with serious stuff like this, there's no room for mistakes.

He unscrewed the cap and peered in. Please be gas I thought in my head. I flipped on the light from my cell phone to help and "Yup all good," Todd said as he screwed the cap back on. "Let's check the sails," he added.

We jumped up on the roof of the cabin and for the first time I pulled off the sail cover that was holding our main sail, nice and tightly wrapped and protected from the elements. I was hoping it had done its job protecting our sail because I hadn't put much thought into it until this moment really.

"Looks alright," he said optimistically as he began raising the sail.

"Looks great!" he said now as the sail reached the top of the mast and fully unfurled, and catching some wind it rocked the whole boat.

"Awesome!" I said, as a weight lifted from my body. Things seemed to be going smooth so far.

"Do you have the front sail?" he asked as he lowered the main sail back down?

"Uuummm I think so maybe," I said clearly unsure. "There's a bunch of bags of different types of sails stuffed in the bathroom. I'm not sure which one it is," I told Todd, which reminded me we had a bathroom at all.

Up until then I had been using the marina's. This one was like a tiny storage closet for sails. Todd knew right away which one it was.

"This is it. Let's bring it out but we don't need it on yet," he said. "You ready to go?" he asked.

I wasn't. But when would I be? I was just trying to take it all in.

"Yes," I said back feeling more serious myself now.

"You sure?" he asked.

It must have been obvious I wasn't.

"Yeah, just run me through how this is going to go," I said clearly a little nervous.

"We untie the boat from the dock. We turn on your little engine. And we get moving," he stated plainly.

"Alright word haha," I said and laughed with relief and that's what we did.

Before I could second guess my decision, Todd was untying the boat.

"Start the engine!" he yelled as he untied the last rope.

I yanked on the pull start and it fired right up, "Yeww!" I shouted and we cheered as he jumped in the boat with me.

There we were, free-floating at the marina away from dock. Time stood still momentarily as I noticed the ripples catching light in the black water that surrounded us.

"You got it?" he asked quickly as I snapped out of it.

"Yeah," I responded.

"You sure?" Todd asked again.

"Yeah I got this," I reassured him, but inside I was freaking out. All I could think was if this dude really even had a boat or knew how to drive one and if anyone was going to hit these other very expensive boats around us in my boat, it better be me.

"K, take us out of here," he said.

"Here we go, hang on tight," I said as I switched the engine from neutral to reverse she jolted back and I adjusted the speed slower like a crawl as I gripped the giant chrome steering wheel with the other hand and looked back over my shoulder sitting at the helm.

"All clear," a voice came from the front of the boat. Todd had run to the bow to tell me what I couldn't see from the back. It was very strange to me how the steering was set up like that, but I guess that's sailing. It involves a crew usually.

Click. Click. The engine switch went as I put it in neutral and quickly into forward as we were steadily approaching some expensive boats in reverse.

"Forward! Forward! Throttle!" he yelled as he ran back to help.

"Oh shit!" I yelled out loud and in my head many times.

Vroooooooooom! The engine roared while trying to stop the reverse momentum and move forward. It was like hitting the breaks, the boat stopped and the water around the engine bubbled and churned as the boat tried to catch some traction in the black liquid.

"Ha ha whoah!" I let out a triumphant laugh.

"Ha ha close one!" he said as he cracked a beer, his short wild hair blowing in the wind. "Sure you don't want one?" Todd asked and he seemed to lighten up as we crept through the marina making our way out into the Bay.

"I'm good, thanks man," I said with a smile.

I am not sure he could even see it was so dark. I was feeling drunk on excitement, it was my first time ever being in the captain's seat of my own sailboat especially one with an engine, the ones I learned on were smaller and nothing like this at all.

He went down into the cabin and I could hear him flipping switches.

"Did that work?" he shouted out from the cabin.

"Na nothing happened, Todd, which way do I go man?" I replied feeling kind of blind suddenly as we exited the marina.

"Keep her straight," he yelled back.

"K," I replied.

"Anything now?" he asked again.

"Naw man. What am I looking for?" I asked.

"The lights," he said shortly, "You have no lights." He sounded really serious again.

"What does that mean?" I asked stupidly.

"It means you have no lights," he replied.

"Do we need them?" I asked.

"You're supposed to, but I guess, fuck it," he added.

"Ha ha, awesome, wait, will we get in trouble?" I asked half happy half concerned about reality.

"If we get caught, but we will just tell him some piece of shit sold you this boat and didn't tell you it was broken. Plus it's a short ride, we won't get caught."

That was good enough for me and we were already on our way. There was really no stopping us now…

Todd went up to the bow and pointed me in the right direction. The journey had just started and already I felt like a pirate living like an outlaw of the sea, travelling in the dead of night on a sea of black with no lights. To passers-by we would have been a ship to be weary of for sure.

Shpop! Went the top of another brew.

"Cheers!" Todd said as he handed me the hash pipe.

"Cheers dude! Wow, thank you so much," I said as I blocked the wind from the pipe and took a big hit.

He smiled back at me, "You're welcome bro, ready to cut the engine?" he asked.

"Let's just go engine power for tonight man I think," I responded. I was just feeling overwhelmed for so long and the steady cruising of the engine felt nice and easy.

"Aw c'mon man, let's bust out the sails!" he exclaimed. He was like a kid in a toy store, he seemed so happy, but what he wasn't telling me was that we didn't even have enough gas for that. We needed to use some wind power.

"Alright let's do it," I said as I killed the engine and he'd already started hoisting the main sail.

"Do you want the front sail?" I shouted up at him.

"Nope, we should be good with just this," he replied.

It was too dark to start attaching sails to lines we couldn't even see.

"Cool," I said as I took another rip off the pipe and let him get us set up.

He was enjoying it and I was absorbing it like a sponge.

"Thanks again, man." I couldn't stop thanking him. "You really are a godsend," I added.

"It's really no problem at all," he said still smiling. I could see the toothless shimmer in the moonlight as he finished raising the sail.

Just then the sail caught a little blast of wind. We were moving again, but this time by the power of nature.

We began moving steady through the night as the moon and its reflections lit the way. It was smooth. We were covering ground, or ocean, whatever, cruising. It was like we knew what we were doing when it all came to a halt.

The noise was something like if you had a plastic bucket over your head and rubbed sandpaper around the outside. It was a long smooth grinding sound as the boat came to a complete stop.

"What the?!" I yelled.

"Oohah," Todd let out some sounds.

"What the fuck just happened?" I yelled.

"We hit a shoal," Todd replied blankly.

"A wha?" I retorted.

"A shoal," Todd said again, "It's like a massive sand bar in the water, a shallow spot created from big dredging ships and sometimes occurring naturally." He added, "We're going to be okay, let me see the engine please if you don't mind," as he swapped places with me and cranked the engine in reverse full throttle.

"What are you doing?!" I asked probably sounding concerned.

"Getting us off this shoal," he yelled now as the engine tried its hardest while sounding like it was struggling in muck. All the feelings of good that had put me at ease were suddenly gone. I thought to myself that it couldn't get worse and like horrible evil magic, it began to rain.

"We've got weather, Joe!" Todd shouted and it all became too real. There was no more fucking around. This wasn't it either, not like this. I snapped into gear, the engine bubbling and splashing as it continued revving at its highest.

"What can I do?" I shouted at Todd still throttling an unmoving engine.

"Stand on the back and bounce," he yelled back as the wind started picking up and the engine roared. Was this a joke?

"Hang on to the lines!" he yelled, so I didn't fall overboard.

"K," I said as I jumped on the stern of the vessel and began a bouncing motion. Something worked.

We were free and the boat began to move as the storm increased. We reversed off the shoal and the storm winds began blowing harder as the boat began leaning to one side. We were really, really moving now. Most boats I think, travel while staying level, like maybe the front will lift if you get good speed or it will lean when you turn, but they stay level for the most part. Sailboats though, they travel leaning to one side while going straight forward if being powered by wind. No one ever tells you that.

There was no time for cheering or rejoicing as Todd continued, "We've got weather, Joe!" he said again sounding very nervous.

Shpop! He cracked open his last beer.

Weren't there six? I thought. Where had the beer gone? Where had the time gone. I was getting nervous, too. He seemed wasted and I watched as he stood on the top of the boat clutching the mast with one hand, chugging his beer with the other, swaying and saying, "We've got weather!" he blasted again as lightning flashed images of his toothless bearded face in the night. Rain now lashing down hard.

"I hear ya, Todd. What do we do?!" I yelled out.

"Keep her straight," he yelled back, but facing forward, his voice getting lost in the wind.

"I'll try," I shouted ahead.

The boat was leaning hard to the right. The wind gusted in from behind us on the left and I could see the lights in the distance but getting closer.

"Is that it?" I yelled.

"Just a little further," he replied. The wind started dying and the rain suddenly stopped.

Todd made his way back to me at the wheel.

"That was awesome wasn't it?" he asked.

"Wild!" I replied, shaking my head, prematurely thinking the ride was over.

"Alright, get ready here," Todd said, serious again.

The lights were in full sight now and we were still heading straight for them.

"What do I do?" I asked.

"Want me to take over?" Todd asked slurring his words.

I hesitated. I did want him to, but was he too drunk? Did he even know what he was doing if he wasn't drunk?

"Uh, I got it I think," I replied hesitantly, the wall of lights now getting closer and closer.

"K slow it down," he said.

And I untied the sail from the cleat by my side letting it loose, the wind that was being caught and propelled us now passed us by.

"Alright", I said and put the motor on and into forward. We were cruising safely and had just embarked on my first voyage in a sailboat.

The wall of light started to warp before my eyes.

"What am I looking at? What are we cruising towards Todd?" I asked him with urgency in my voice.

"It's a waterway, a canal straight ahead, slow it down" Todd said trying to see where we were too, "Yup this is it! Steady now" he said.

There were lights now on either side of us as we entered the canal slowly. The wall of lights had opened up and begun to wrap around us, I couldn't see much but it looked like a dead end.

"You sure Todd dude?" I asked.

He was at the bow now letting me know where to go. Since the squall was gone, the night became much more silent again and we could hear each other clearly.

"Of course!" he said, now searching for what I guess must be his dock.

"Left!" he blasted unexpectedly.

"Left!?" I yelled back.

"Now!" he said and I whipped a hard left and realized we were six feet from a wall now on my right.

"Holy shit!" I said as I put the engine in neutral and we spun in a circle slowly.

"Haha it's ok" Todd laughed out.

"Bro do you know where we are, really?" I asked now, very seriously as we floated in the dark.

"It's right up ahead, I promise" Todd tried to assure me. I wasn't sure of anything he said now, but he had kinda gotten us this far.

"Alright, I'm gonna cruise up slow, you point it out," I was just trying to communicate basic plans at this point in case he was really wasted. We were now creeping down the waterway slowly, searching for his dock, but even slowly moving boats are hard to stop.

"Oops there it is" he said "kick it in neutral" Todd added, so I did, but the boat still had pretty good momentum.

"Oops there it goes" he said, as we passed it, "Reverse!" he shouted as I quickly changed gears. The engine created an undertoe of whirling water until the propeller caught, and we went from a pause to a reverse motion. I saw the little dock on my right and slammed the engine forward and turned the boat hard right and right into the dock space and back into reverse as we nearly hit the wall and Todd jumped off onto the dock and caught the boat before any damage could be done.

"Woah good job!" he yelled joyfully as I shut off the engine.

"Thanks man" I replied somberly. I was exhausted, not from the time of night but from the thoughts in my own head, once again, well maybe the time too.

4:19 AM, I could see it on his digital watch glowing.

"Well we're here, we made it, wanna smoke a goodnight bowl and hit the hay?" he asked.

"Hell yeah, where are you sleeping?" I responded and asked rudely. I was just curious, like were we docked at his house or something? "I mean you're welcome to sleep on here with me, I was just wondering where your house was" I said trying not to sound rude.

"Right there brother" he said pointing to a sailboat in the dark at a spot next to us on the dock, "That's mine," he added, "my house is like ten minutes away."

He really had the same fucking boat, we smoked a bowl and said goodnight. He went onto his boat and I passed out there on mine.

DAY 3

The warm orange glow of the morning sun gently hit my face through the porthole window on the side of the boat. I smiled with my eyes still closed as I heard the squawking of seagulls. That was like a crazy nightmare mixed with a dream, and I had made it out alive. I opened my eyes, stood up and stretched while breathing in the salty fresh air. I felt accomplished, like I had achieved a goal. This boat, our boat was awesome, it needed some work, but it was great and I felt more comfortable with her now. I took a little wake and bake hit off the pipe still sitting there with some hash and some herb and went to see where I was now docked.

"Oh shit" I said out loud and to myself as I looked at the rundown dock I was sitting at. The wooden boards were broken and rotten and falling into a large hole that looked like someone had fallen through already.

"That's why it's free" Todd said and smiled as he popped up out of his boat docked next to mine.

"Haha hey goodmorning" I said

"Morning" he said

"Wait so this is yours or we're just using it?" I asked.

"I work here at this marina and they let me use these two condemned docks" Todd said.

"So awesome" I said looking around noticing it wasn't a normal marina I had been used to, it was more like boat storage on a creek. There weren't boats all around on docks they were on land stacked on top of each other in like a parking garage for boats. It looked very industrial around me.

"I actually gotta go to work now but you're good to stay here as long as you need" Todd said.

"Todd man, my brotha, thank you so much, this is great" I replied.

"You're welcome man that was fun, come over and find me at work if you need me, or anything" he said.

"That was crazy man, alright, thanks I will" I said as he started off towards work. I needed to get to work too but I had no idea where to start.

The sun blazed high in the sky now and it was a bright beautiful day with a calmness in the light breeze that cooled me down. I called everyone to let them know I was alright, realizing I probably should have texted when I got in last night or early this morning but they were probably sleeping anyway. Told my mom it was smooth sailing but I told the boys how crazy it really was. I was on facetime with Sean and he was with Dave and Booger, no surprise.

"And then SMASH!" I said making a crashing noise with my mouth, "we hit something and it started storming hard and Todd was belligerently screaming ""we've got weather Joe"" but the boats fine," I spewed out like I couldn't say it fast enough, "well except a few things, the lights and the centerboard but it came like that" I added

"Fuuuck," Dave said dragged out.

"Shit dude, we have no more money for now," Sean said.

"Knew this was a bad idea," Booger said as he turned away from the phone.

"I know it sucks but we should have expected this, I will take care of it guys," I said

"Alright I got faith," Dave said.

"Same it'll be all good," Sean said

"Yeah, we'll let you know if we get more money," Dave said, "and send us your location," he added.

"Word, sorry dudes but it's a great boat, everything's gonna work out I think," I said.

"Hope so," Booger boogered and we all said "Peace Out" and other ways to say bye.

As I hung up the phone and looked around I knew it was up to me to make this right and get the boat ready to search for Sensemilla Island.

Ten seconds or ten minutes maybe passed as I daydreamed my plan of action when a large object started cruising into my peripheral and up the creek towards me. It was a vessel that looked an awful lot like the one Todd and I had but much larger. On the bow stood a strange character shirtless with a big belly and a little speedo.

"Grab the lines," he yelled as he cruised passed slowly, tossing me the ropes to tie up his ship.

"Where should I," I started to yell out to him.

"Anywhere," he stopped me, "just don't let go," he said and he began maneuvering this large sailboat that seemed like it was too big for the waterway, into a dock spot and I tied his lines to the dock.

"Thank you sir," he said emerging from his ship wearing pants now.

"No prob," I said back, "Is that an Irwin?" I asked.

"Tis indeed Boy O," he said, "you know yer boats aye?" he added.

"I know that type of boat because mine is one also and so is my friends there," I said as I pointed to the two sailboats next to us.

"That's strange," he said.

"Yeah I thought they were pretty rare," I said.

"They are and great vessels as well," he replied, "name's Gill," he added.

"Joe," I said still bewildered by this odd coincidence and we shook hands, "Looks like we got a little army of them," I said.

"Haha," he laughed and climbed back onto his ship, "You hungry?" he asked out of nowhere catching me off guard.

"Yeah!" I exclaimed. I'd forgotten about food again with mind occupied by the thoughts of preparing for a journey somehow.

"Follow me," he said climbing back onto his boat.

"Awesome!" I said and followed.

We got onto his ship and it was a smelly mess with piles of junk but it was really cool with lots of old interesting things like nautical instruments and maps everywhere. We stepped down into the belly of the beast where we took a seat at something like a dining room table, with bench seats or booths that could probably be converted into a full size bed. Like I said, his vessel was much much larger than our own. Without hesitation he pulled out some saltine crackers and two cans of sardines. My jovial smile went flat and my brows lifted in my natural response to seeing this. He must have noticed my change of attitude because he peeled back the tin lid and held it up towards my face and said, "Come on! It's boat food."

Boat food? Boat food? I thought as my stomach let out a growl like an angry dog protecting me.

"Uhh, I'm not high enough for that," I said, "but I really appreciate it man," I added.

"High enough?" Gill pulled the can back and perked up, "you have herbs?" he asked with extreme curiosity.

"Yeah man, I'll go grab real quick," I said.

"Alright, go, go" he said and motioned with his hands.

I climbed up and out of the massive sailboat, jumped down to the dock and ran to my boat, grabbed Todd's wooden pipe and put what was left of the gram in the bowl. It wasn't much but it would have to do. The sun wasn't as high in the sky anymore and I remembered I was on a mission but it felt like another day was slipping by. I returned on to Gill's boat to find he didn't need to be high to eat, he was face deep in canned fish.

"Yo ho," I said like a pirate.

"Ahoy mate," he said back continuing the pirate banter, "did yee find the magical herb?" he asked.

"Eye, I did but there not be much," I replied.

Damn we sounded like real pirates I thought to myself as I handed him the pipe and lighter.

"Looks good to me," he said as he went in for the hit.

We shared the bowl back and forth as we learned a little about each other and how we got there, I didn't mention Sensemilla Island yet. Gill worked around the corner in the bay at another marina taking people out on tours. He had just acquired this boat from an old man who could no longer sail, for one dollar, he said. Over the last few days or week, whatever it was, I had gotten a crash course in boats, so to say. Hearing he had gotten this large beautiful ship for a dollar was shocking but I had come to find from reading, research, and things people said at docks that, B.O.A.T. really meant, "Bust Out Another Thousand," as in thousand dollars to repair and constant upkeep for boats. So for people that know this, the reality of the boat market is, that it can be hard to even give a boat away, let alone sell it when you need to.

"Mmm that be some good tweeds," Gill said smoke now billowing from his mouth as he spoke.

"Eye," I said and we shared some laughs, finished the rest of the bowl and said goodnight.

"Great meeting ya Gill," I said as I climbed down off his ship.

"Same here bud, see ya tomorrow, neighbor," Gill replied from the top deck, "and thanks for the toke," he added.

"Anytime brudda," I yelled back stepping onto my boat and crawling into the cabin.

I was tired but I needed to come up with a plan still. A storm of thoughts filled my stoney mind. How can I get this boat ready for the sea? Should I get a job around here to pay for parts? Where are my friends? Was this a mistake? And with that final thought I was out like a light that my boat needed to replace.

DAY 4

"Joe we've got weather" I could hear Todd yelling while the boat rocked violently back and forth. I couldn't see a thing, was this a nightmare? My eyes snapped open and I jumped to my feet, back into ready position.

"You in there Boy O," Gill's voice called and I could hear Todd laughing. They must have met and he told him the story, so they were shaking the boat.

"You Fucks," I shouted, "I'm here," I said as I emerged laughing. I felt like I'd known these guys forever already, there they were, couple of goofballs both standing on the dock laughing.

"Aye!" and "Hey!" they both cheered.

"The Irwin crew," I yelled out as I gestured at our three rare boats in a row. We all cheered. The vibes were great, the sun was up, and it was a beautiful day.

My pocket buzzed and a text on the lock-screen read,

Dave: [We're selling shit, to get shit]

Dave: [You in?]

I opened up my phone,

Me: [YES!]

I replied.

Me: [Stop by my place]

I called home and asked my mom if she could round up a few things and give them to my friends when they came by.

Then texted the boys again,

Me: [There will be stuff ready for you to grab when you get there]

Sean: [Word]

Dave: [Cool]

Me: [Awesome thanks]

This would either help fix the boat or get a bunch of bud if it all sold. I told my mom to grab my trading cards binder, my ipad, and my beautiful long-board surfboard.

"What's happening, any plans?" Todd asked clapping his hands together ready for another adventure it seemed, with a big smile on his face as usual.

"Feeling good," I said as I stepped onto the dock joining Todd and Gill, leaving the boat rocking behind me, "thought I might have to get a job around here to buy stuff for the boat but my friends, the rest of the crew, are selling our stuff today so we can buy stuff." I said with relief and a smile on my face as well.

"Don't sell anything if you don't want to" Todd said more seriously suddenly, "I was thinking last night and you can have anything off my boat that your boat needs to be seaworthy" he added.

"WOAH!" Gill said quickly.

"Woah," I repeated, "Todd dude, I can't do that man, that's too kind."

I meant it too, but I wanted it so bad.

"I won't be sailing anytime soon, I've got work to do here, no time for adventure yet." Todd said, pretty straight up.

"That's one hell of a deal mate," Gill said.

"You sure Todd dude?" I asked.

"Yeah man it'll be fun working on the boat together," Todd said enthusiastically.

"Alright man!" I shouted and jumped with joy, "Dude you're the best!", I yelled at Todd and one-arm hugged him. It felt like we were all cheering. Gill had gotten in Todd's boat and was looking at the lights on the front and sides.

"Yeah this should work perfectly," Gill said.

"Woohoo!" I let out a yell, "it's official Todd dude I will never be able to thank you enough, but THANK YOU!" I exclaimed, and we worked on the boat for the rest of the day switching light covers and bulbs, from one boat to another. Everything was a perfect match, and by the time night fell again, it was complete.

Todd flipped some switches and the boat lit up like a Christmas tree, red lights, yellow lights, blue, and white lights. A beautiful sight to behold and a great feeling knowing the boat was complete and all I needed now was my crew.

I was starving and wanted to smoke by this time when,

"You guys hungry?", Gill asked.

"Starving," I replied.

"Sure, what you got?" Todd asked.

"Please don't say sardines man, please," I laughed but I'd eat anything at that point.

"Be right back," Gill said and he ran to his boat and came back with a little portable grill and a cooler.

"Anymore smoke Joe?" Todd asked as he stood and watched Gill set up a kitchen on the dock.

"Na man I wish, but my friends should be bringing some," I said.

"Oh ok, I've got more hash here if you'd like?" Todd said.

"WHAT!? YES please!" I replied extatically.

Gill's ears perked up too and he looked at Todd wide eyed, "Well what are we waiting for?" Gill asked, "You fire up the hash, I'll fire up the steak," he said as he pulled meat and beer out of the cooler, "Anyone want a beer?" he added.

"Ok haha yeah," Todd said simply and I just looked at the heavens in bewilderment of how this was all happening this way. The boat, the weed, the people, it was all too good to be true.

The night went on as we smoked, drank and ate, the light of the fire flickered on our faces from the little grill as we talked around it. Gill told us how people leave stuff everyday at his job with the intent for it to be thrown away and he gets to keep it all, all types of drinks and food. We were chilling for sometime when out of nowhere, "You must be pretty tough," Gill asked me.

"Huh?" I responded confused, Todd just sat there eating and drinking quietly.

"You've gotta be tough to be a captain," Gill said starring me down, his eyes glowing orange from the fire.

"Captain? I guess I didn't think of it like that," I said.

"C'mere let's see what yer made of," Gill said slurring as he stood up. We were about the same size, he's just a little heavier and a little older.

"Oh you want a piece of me!?" I said making my way around the fire and into his face smiling.

"Don't even try it BoyO," he said as he pushed me back with two fingers to the chest and it was on. We were locked in a grip, pushing and slamming each other around. Todd watched like it was dinner and a movie as we made our way wrestling onto my boat. I threw him down, he kicked me away and I backed into something sharp.

"AAgh!" I let out a yell and dove on him unleashing some body punches.

"AAgh!" he let one out too, "Alright Alright I'm done, you're tough," he said as he gave up, and I pulled him up to his feet.

"You good?" I asked laughing.

"Yeah, I got some hernia surgery recently," he said.

"Oh fuck, my bad dude, you shouldn't have started with me," I said half sorry.

"You're bleeding" Todd said calmly.

"Who!? Where!?" Gill said worried it was him.

"Joe," Todd said, "on your back," he added.

I must have hit something sharp in the dark on my boat.

"Is it bad?" I asked as I lifted my shirt.

"Naaah, just a scrape," Gill said.

"Cool," I said as I pulled my shirt back down, "You guys wanna hear some music?" I asked.

"Yeah," Todd said.

"Does a shark shit in the sea?" Gill said, "Can I play the drum?" he added.

"You play?" I asked.

"No, but I'll try," he replied and I got him the djembe and I played the guitar and we jammed nonsense songs till the sun came up. It woke Todd, who had fallen asleep in a beach chair from one of the boats.

"What's happening?" Todd asked sleepily, Gill was already boarding his ship for bed.

"What's happening is we partied all night and now it's time to sleep a little," I said to Todd.

"Night," Gill yelled back as went down into his cabin.

"Night brutha," I yelled back.

"Goodnight," Todd replied and he went into his boat.

It's the pirates life for me, I thought to myself as I went and laid in my boat.

DAY 5

I don't think much time had passed when I heard the familiar sounds of Booger whinning.

"Are you sure this is it?" Booger said.

It was him, I was actually excited to hear Booger complain, I never thought I'd see the day.

"GUYS!" I shouted at them as I bounced off the boat and over to the rusty fence they were on the other side of.

There was the canal, the wooden docks of different sizes, and a thin piece of land with bits of old asphalt exposed among the overgrown grass, basically a path to the boat docks, lined by this fence with trees and shrubs grown through it. The trees and foliage thinned out near the gate entrance and that's where I met them.

"Brooo," Sean and Dave yelled simultaneously, they weren't twins, but sometimes act like it.

Booger was there too, "yellow," he said.

They had bags on their backs and things in their hands, I was stoked to say the least.

"Hold on let me get the key from Todd," I said and turned to Todd's boat and went in to find him face down on a bench.

"Dude! Dude!" I shook him, "Can I get the key to the fence? My friends are here!" I tried not to shout in his face, but I was excited.

"Sure here, but let me get it right back though," Todd groaned still half asleep.

"Thanks," I said and ran back out to let me friends in, "Duuuudes!" I said as I opened the gate.

"Yaaay!" we all kind of said as we cheered and bumped fists and hugged.

I let them in and was about to close it when I thought, "Where'd you guys park?" I asked.

"Up the street at the fast food place," Booger replied.

"Fast food!?" I said, no surprise I was hungry again. I hadn't even left the dock yet and ventured out to see what was around me. Dave and Sean nodded as if to say, yep lets do it.

"Alright drop your shit on the boat and let's go!" I said.

"Is it safe?" Booger asked.

"What do you mean?", I asked slightly offended for no reason, "Safe?" I added.

"I mean it looks like kind of a sketchy area," Booger boogered.

I didn't think of it like that but yeah, I guess he was right.

"It's fine, plus Todd and Gill are here," I answered.

"You trust them?" Booger snapped back, "with all this?" He opened a back pack to reveal at least a pound of weed.

"Oh fuck!" I said covering the bag with my hand, "close it up, yeah it'll be fine, let's just put it away and lock up the boat," I said. The boys all looked at me, "It's fine," I repeated.

It was just a combination lock that held the two rickity wooden cabin doors locked but I trusted no one would hop the fence to break into our dingey looking sailboat, probably owned by poor vagrants, and if they did, they'd get caught by Todd, Gill, or someone that worked there. We locked up the boat locked the gate, and went and got food. Fast food is life honestly, a burger with lettuce, cheese, and tomato for a dollar is unbeatable. We sat and ate and they told me about how they sold all our stuff and bought the weed, a GPS, flare gun, flares, a radio, and we had some money left, plus Booger's dad had a membership to one of those giant grocery stores like a warehouse you buy food in bulk at and we had a bag of rice, lots of canned chicken, tuna, corn and handles of liquor. Some of it was still in the car so we finished eating, drove down to the fence and unloaded onto the boat. I couldn't believe what they had done, even Booger was down. This was really happening. They even brought some surfboards, more instruments, and our own little gas powered grill with propane cans, we were set.

"Eye, who goes there?" a voice shouted at us. It was light out still and Gill could see from his boat, it was me clearly.

"Guys this is Gill. Gill this is Sean, Dave, and Booger," I said pointing each one out to Gill who was making his way over to us.

"Booger aye?" he questioned, "Must be a real turd" he said, already messing with the boys. Booger looked at me like I said something to Gill about him. I just put my hands up and laughed, "He's fucking with you, he's an ass" I said.

"An ass!?" he blasted back, "Is that how yee thank me for the steak dinner?" he asked half joking and winked and punched my shoulder.

"Yeah yeah," I grinned. The boys looked left-out of an inside joke or something. "He's gunna trya and toughen us up guys," I elbowed Sean, "Get ready," I said.

"I've got to prepare you for the sea," Gill said.

"Shut up," I said laughing, "Let's go smoke," I added, and with that we all went to our boat to smoke together for the first time as a crew.

Todd eventually came over and joined us and I gave him the key back. It was a full boat and it was full of smoke pouring out every porthole. I believe we were christening the boat.

"Where's your dinghy?" Gill called out through the smoke, followed by some coughs.

"Dinghy!?" Sean repeated loudly, laughing hysterically. Like children the crew erupted in laughter, Booger was in good spirits too, but we noticed Todd and Gill looking at us seriously, no longer laughing.

"You have no dinghy, mate?" Gill asked again.

"You need a life-boat Joe or you'll get in trouble out there."

Buzzkill, the mood changed drastically but we were all being pretty cool about it. I was about to speak up but was still holding a hit so if I tried it would have been mumbled anyway.

"Yeah, I read something about that," Booger said in a kinda chill way.

"Oh word, what did it say?" I finally chimed in.

"Says we need one," Booger said.

"Shit, how much will it be?" I said looking at Gill or Todd for the answer.

"They can be pretty pricey with insurance," Todd said.

"Depends," said Gill.

"Depends on what?" Booger and I both asked.

"If you get it new or used and if you insure it," Gill replied.

"What do you mean, if? Don't we have to insure it?" Booger asked.

"Used sounds nice," I said.

"Free sounds nicer though doesn't it?" Gill said.

"Free?!" I said back.

"Don't you need to insure dinghy's here?" Booger repeated, ignoring the new conversation.

"Yeah I thought so too," Todd said about the insurance.

"People leave busted and deflated dinghy's at my marina every once in a while, I can try and find one that looks salvageable and no, you don't have to insure it if you paint on the side of it, "T/T" followed by your boat name. Which means, Tender To, and you're only using it to travel to and from the sailboat," Gill said like it was no big deal but he may have just saved us a ton of money.

Meanwhile Sean and Dave were passing the pipe and talking about something else all together, laughing.

"Did not know that myself," Todd said.

"DUDE! That would be a life saver," I said.

"Like, literally," Booger laughed.

"It's not a definite but I'll try," Gill said.

We all continued smoking and joking for a little longer till we realized Booger fell asleep on the long bench, and the good spots started getting called. They had, had a long drive to get there.

"Other bench!" Sean shouted as he jumped on it.

"Triangle thing!" Dave said, talking about the front main cabin bed area. I wanted them to be comfortable, it was their first night still. There were still two long benches out on deck by the steering wheel and the boat could be slept all over really, right on the roof of the cabin or bow, if I wanted.

"We brought the hammock," Dave said.

"Oh nice, I'll take that," I said. Todd and Gill started making their way off our boat and towards their own.

"Night BoyO's," Gill yelled back.

"Night," Todd said.

"Night," we all yelled back except Booger who was sleeping through it all. I hung the hammock right through the center of the cabin and it became the new best spot.

"That's sick!" Dave said.

"Yeah," Sean said, "we need more hammock," he added trying to get comfortable on the short bench.

"We can rotate sleep spots," I said leaning over and turning off the cabin lights. "See ya in the morning mates," I added and passed out and then was woken back up after it felt like I had just shut my eyes.

"JOE! JOE!," someone said shacking my hammock rapidly back and forth. It was Booger, "Something's happening man, wake up," he whispered.

That got my attention and I was instantly wide awake, "What is it Booger?" I whispered back, our faces glowing from his cell phone's LED screen.

"You hear that?!" he let out a scratchy whispering yell quietly and then paused to listen.

"Oh ha ha," I laughed softly realizing what he was hearing. It was that strange crackling sound coming from under the boat.

"Yeah man it's like roaches or something," I laughed.

"Roaches!" he yelled. "Oh fuck, no!" he yelled again.

"What's happening?" said Dave who woke up from the commotion.

"Roaches, man, and not the good kind," I said, "Go back to bed and we'll deal with it later," I added trying to get back to sleep.

"No way, man, are you sure?" Booger asked, "How do you know it's roaches?" he went on.

"I saw a couple but I'm not 100 percent sure," I said.

"That sounds louder than roaches," Dave said.

"We'll figure it out tomorrow," I said and went back to sleep.

DAY 6

When I woke up the boys were already up. Booger was cooking on the grill. Dave was fishing in the creek. And Sean was rolling a fat blunt. The day was starting off right to say the least.

"You guys sleep good?" I asked most likely knowing the answer.

"Not at all," Booger replied straight up. "I felt something fat crawling on my neck and grabbed it and threw it, pretty sure it was a roach," Booger added.

"Eh, wasn't too bad, definitely doable," Dave said.

"Was good for me, fell asleep to like the motion of the ocean," Sean said.

"Ha ha well good," I said to all of them laughing out loud. "Now you know how I been living," I said smiling.

The small boat was busy with our activity everyone getting familiar with the vessel and the sun was shining.

"Ahoy!" Gill yelled from his boat in a bright colored Speedo.

"Yo!" I yelled back.

"Dude's a weirdo," Booger said.

"Dude's a legend," I said. "And he might help us if you're lucky," I added in a matter-of-fact way.

"Legend?" Dave asked.

"Yeah man, Gill's a fucking legend," I said.

They all looked at me stopping what they were doing to listen.

"This dude lassoed a dolphin when he needed propulsion he got it from a porpoise. The Kracken himself avoids Gilly at sea. And, he fucks mermaids!" I said.

"None of that's true," Booger said abruptly.

"Oh really!" Gill's voice came from out of nowhere. He was now standing on our dock that appeared to crumble under his feet it was so weathered.

Booger looked startled, "I mean, it can't be? Can it, sir?" Booger said squirming.

"Morning, Gill," I said, and the boys repeated.

"Morning BoyO's," he said to us but he was intently focused on Booger now. "Every word of it," he said very seriously to Booger. "Alright everyone, what's your plan for today?" he asked smiling, changing the subject.

The boys all looked around at each other, "I'm gonna try and get this center board working," I said, not sure if I had even told them about this problem yet.

"There's no trying, there's only doing," Gill said.

"What's a center board?" Dave asked as he passed me the blunt.

"It's this giant fin for our boat and it's heavy, to keep us from blowing over when the wind is strong and keep us moving straight," I had just looked it up on my phone.

"What's wrong with it?" Booger asked concerned.

"It's stuck," I said.

"Can we just sail without it?" Sean asked.

"Todd said we could, but others said not to," I said, and then yelled over at his boat, "TODD!" but no answer.

"He went to work, and he's an idiot," Gill said.

"Ha ha, great guy though," I said trying to lighten it back up.

"Yeah great guy but, you need your center board," Gill said, and he was right.

"So how do we fix it?" Dave asked.

"Carefully," Gill said, "You don't want to snap the line in there," Gill added.

There was a thin rope built in, used to raise and lower the center board as needed.

"I think I got it, I'm gunna go down and scrape off the barnacles, hopefully that's all it is," I said.

"Okay, nice," Sean said, still puffing on the fatty that was getting smaller.

I was in my bathing suit and goggles ready to go down with my knife in hand and start picking away, but Gill said, "Hold on, I should warn you that as you scrape, it releases stuff, small creatures and sea lice that attack while you're down there and even still be itchy after."

"Oh now ya tell me, well that sucks," I said, "But it's gotta be done," I added preparing to get in the water which was warm and clear so that wasn't a problem. It was the thought of the little creatures in my dreadlocks that bothered me, but it did have to be done.

I pulled my goggles down over my eyes and started climbing down the ladder on the back of the boat and into the creek.

"Going for a swim?" I heard Todd's voice as I was just going under.

I popped back up, "Hey Todd, haha na, gunna try and free up the, I'm going down to free up the center board," I said correcting myself. "There was no more 'trying' only doing," I could hear Gill's voice in my head and I went to plunge back under.

"Wait!" Todd shouted and I popped back up.

"I got permission to use the forklift to take your boat out of the water so we can clean her up and work on her on land," Todd said.

"For free?" Gill asked for us and maybe for him.

"Yeah!" Todd replied excitedly.

Right away I wasn't sure. Things were going good the way they were and I was about to fix it anyway, but I liked free stuff and I wanted to do what's best for the boat and the boys.

"That's usually like $800.00," Gill said, looking at me and the crew.

"Shit, let's do it," Dave said.

"I dunno guys, I'm already down here ready to do what needs to be done," I said, "And plus, a forklift?" I added.

"That's how it's done," Todd said more seriously now, "But if you don't want to I'll tell my work nevermind," Todd said.

I felt an opportunity slipping by but for some reason it just wasn't feeling right.

"We should do it," Booger said, "It's free and it's something other boaters do, let's just do it," he continued.

"A forklift though?" I repeated.

"It's what they use for smaller boats," Todd said.

"Alright let's do it," I said, trying to sound confident, but it was the first time so far I was going with the flow but against my gut.

"Bring your boat over to the main dock, I'll be there waiting with the lift," Todd said.

"K, up the way?" I said and pointed asking.

"Yep, just up the creek," Todd yelled back as he jogged back into the boat yard.

"Hang on men," I shouted, as I fired up the engine.

"See you later," Gill said. He hopped off the boat.

"Later," I yelled at him and threw it in reverse and whipped out of the dock spot and back into forward. I was driving the sailboat like a speed boat.

"Whoah!" Booger and Dave let out a yell.

"Ha ha, yes," Sean said as he stumbled a little climbing up to the bow.

"Lemme know if there's anything I don't see up there, Sean," I shouted up ahead.

"K," he yelled back and we were off on our first mini-voyage together in our boat. Just a short one upstream, but still. I could see the excitement in their eyes as they looked down at the passing water. We were only going like two miles an hour, but in a boat, it feels like twenty miles per hour.

"There's Todd," Sean yelled back and I put the engine in neutral and started slowing down. I could see Todd now, too. He was waving us in, hanging out the side of a big forklift on the edge of a dock.

"Bring it in here slowly," Todd yelled.

"Straight in?" I shouted at Todd.

"Yup," he replied. "Nice and easy," he added.

Alright, here goes nothing, I thought to myself as I lined up the boat with the giant padded forks of the lift and eased it in smoothly.

"Hey, hey!" I said, celebrating the move.

"Perfect," Todd said and told everyone to get off and grab anything breakable that could get messed up when it's getting lifted.

We just grabbed the pipe and some weed and hopped off.

"Looks so sketchy," Booger said to the group.

"Todd, you're sure about this right?" I asked.

"Yes, I do it all the time for boats this size," he replied.

"What about for bigger boats?" I asked.

"We use the straps," he replied.

"The straps?" Booger asked.

"Yes, large fabric straps that go around the boat and attach to the forks above the boat so it can be pulled up out of the water," he explained.

"Maybe we should do that, I can just back her out and we can strap her up," I said.

"No the boat's going to be fine, I do this all the time," he said again more emphatically.

"Word, I'm just worried, but you know what's up," I said.

"It's fine. This is how it's done," he repeated getting into the driver's seat of the forklift.

"Alright, you're the man. Thank you!" I shouted as he turned on the forklift and we all stood back watching our boat that had begun levitating out of the water like magic. It rained glistening droplets of sun-soaked water from the hull. Time seemed to be slowing while we all gazed at the absurd scene. A sudden jerk and a pop sound broke the enchantment and I screamed, "Put it back! Put it back in!"

"Why? What?" Todd yelled over the engine of the forklift.

"That didn't sound right," I said.

"What really?" Todd replied.

"Yes, seriously!" I shouted and Todd put her back in the water.

"Get the straps," I shouted. "I think you popped a hole in her!" I yelled.

"No way," Todd said.

"Yes fucking way, Todd, dude. I appreciate your help, but I think we got a problem," I exclaimed.

The guys just stood and looked dumbfounded.

"What do we do? Is this a joke?" Booger asked not looking happy.

"Be right back," Todd said, sadly as he ran to get the straps. "Someone come with me, they're heavy," he added.

"Sean, Dave, go with him. Me and Booger will stay with the boat," I said and they followed Todd running.

A moment later they were back with these large yellow fabric straps. They looked like big fire hoses or something.

"Grab this end and bring it around the front, then hand it back to me," Todd yelled at Sean. "You do the same with this one, but around the stern," Todd shouted at Dave.

I stood watch over the operation, ready to jump in wherever it needed.

They fed the yellow strap under the boat and rejoined the ends of the straps together above the boat and slid the loops on the end of the straps onto the forks of the lift. Todd jumped back into the seat of the forklift and shouted, "Ready?!"

I took a last look around, "Yes," I yelled.

We all jumped off the boat and Todd began lifting again. The boat was now being lifted out of the creek, dangling by these yellow straps and clear as day was the hole that Todd had just put in the side of our vessel. I was overwhelmed with so many different feelings. After everything I'd been through already for it to come to an end like this, I was sad. I was frustrated. Tired. Hungry. And in disbelief. All I could do was try my hardest not to be mad because I was the one who agreed to do this and because Todd had helped us so much and got us to this point I'd be lost without him.

"Fuck, dude," I said, completely deflated.

"What!" Todd said but he knew it.

The pressure from the fork on the old fiberglass hull of the boat had pierced her through and water and sludge were leaking like blood as if she was alive.

"NO," Todd got out of the fork lift and came running to see what I was looking at. "Fuck," he yelled confirming what I thought was a problem. "You sure I did that?" he asked, really hoping I wasn't sure.

"Yeah, dude, it fucking jerked and popped and that's when I yelled," I said sure as hell that's what happened, and I understood he didn't want it to be his fault for many reasons, but I knew it was and it had to be for one main reason, we couldn't fix this now without his help and his connections to the marina and boat parts. He knew it too though.

"Alright, I'm going to fix this," he said. "Let me go tell the office what happened. I'll be right back," he said and ran off while the boat still hung lifelessly in the air, dripping and leaking no longer a glorious but grotesque sight to behold.

"What the fuck, Bro," Booger let out as Todd was far enough away.

"I don't know, man," I replied obviously not happy either.

Sean and Dave each lit a cig and walked away from all the action.

"What are we gunna do now?" Booger asked.

"I don't know," I repeated. "Let's just hope Todd can help us out," I added.

"Oh like he just did? And what if he can't?" Booger asked.

"I don't know, man, we'll figure it out," I said not even sure if it was true myself anymore.

That's when Todd came running back over, "Good news?" I asked.

"No, we gotta get your boat outta here actually. They don't want me messing with it here anymore," he replied.

"You're joking," I asked seriously as my stomach dropped.

"Nope, but I gotta plan," Todd said, "I have a friend with a boat junkyard further up the creek. He's got a lift and I know he will let us work on it there!" he said with a smile.

"Bro, there's a hole in my boat," I said as if he didn't get it.

"It'll be fine once we get it there. It's not far at all," he said.

I felt like I was at the will of the world. There really was no other option once again.

"Let's go then," I said.

"You sure 'bout this?" Booger asked me quietly.

"No," I said back to him and with that Todd began lowering our wounded vessel back into the creek as the day slipped by. We undid the straps and I fired her up.

"All aboard," I yelled and the crew plus Todd jumped in and I started her up the creek steadily.

"How far, Todd?" I asked.

"Not far," he replied as we cruised up the canal passing docks and boats on either side.

"There it is on the right," he pointed at a dock and I pulled up like a pro while Todd and Booger jumped out to tie her down.

"Let's be quick she's taking on water somewhere," I said to Todd who was running to find the owner of this boat yard.

"Vinnie!" he yelled out. "Vinnie!" and a small tanned weathered man came running out.

"Whatsa the matta?" he yelled back with an accent.

"I need a favor right now. Can you lift their boat out with straps please. I just put a hole in it," Todd begged.

"You put a hole in it?" he repeated. "Oh Todd, you dummy!" he said. Meanwhile, the boat is sitting in the creek I imagine beginning to flood.

"Please help us," I asked him.

"Okay okay," and he started running for equipment.

He came back with straps and we did the whole thing all over again. Feeding the straps around the hull and again she was raised up out of the water and this time placed on land, supported by beams and propped up so we could fix her I guess.

Sean, Dave, Booger, Todd and I looked at the beautiful ship like it was in a hospital bed and not doing well. Hope and excitement for a journey seemed lost.

"It's gonna be alright, guys. We will fix this and be on our way voyaging," I said trying to bring some optimism back.

"You have 24 hours," boat yard owner Vinnie blurted out.

"Oh come on, Vinnie, we need more time," Todd pleaded.

"No, I told you stop helping people and bring them here," Vinnie angrily shouted in broken English.

"Vinnie, I broke their boat," Todd said.

"How dis my problem?" Vinnie asked.

"Come on, for me, Vinnie, please," Todd asked.

"Okay but this the last time, 48 hours," Vinnie said.

"Alright, thank you. Thank you," Todd said.

"Thank you," we all said and Vinnie left us.

"48 hours?" I turned to Todd and asked. "Is that gonna be enough time?" I added."

"Should be, I'm going to get the stuff right now and be right back," Todd said, "Just wait on the boat," he added and we all went up into the boat that was now propped up on dry land.

"Well this day got crazy," Dave said, as we all convened in the cabin.

"Haha yeah," Sean laughed. Me and Booger didn't say much, I think we were both thinking. I just let out a sigh and said, "Sorry guys, I tried."

"It's alright, man, we know," Dave said passing me the pipe. I didn't know if it was okay to smoke there and I didn't care. I was feeling like I let everyone down, getting us into this mess. I held the pipe in front of my face. Lit the lighter and stared at the flame then proceeded to take the fattest hit I took in days and held it in. By the time I let it out my worries were over and I found a new confidence in the silver lining.

"Hey, maybe we can get the center board moving while we have her like this," I said and grabbed the knife picking up where I left off, climbing down to pick away at the barnacles, but at least this time no creatures and lice to worry about swimming in my hair. The barnacles weren't even on the center board, it was just covering the place the center board was supposed to drop from. I started picking away and it was soon clear enough for the center board.

"Let her down slow if you can," I yelled up onto the boat at whoever was standing near the center board release.

"K!" Sean yelled back.

Woosh! Whack! Were the noises it made as it flew out smoothly and hit the ground.

"Well, that worked," I said. "Maybe slower next time though," I added laughing to myself.

"Oops!" I heard Sean say.

"Is it good?" Booger shouted.

"Looks good to me," I shouted back.

"Aye! We did something right," Dave yelled.

"Ha ha!" Sean blasted laughing.

"Good job! Crank it back up," I said and they did. I felt a glimmer of hope come back.

"Eye eye, Captain," Sean yelled.

"We got this," I shouted, the energy seemed to have returned to the crew as well.

"Got the stuff!" Todd came shouting, running down the driveway with buckets and tools in both hands and a towel over his shoulders.

"NICE!" we all yelled.

"That was fast," I said. "And look, we got the center board working!" I added joyfully.

"Whoah! Good going," he said out of breath.

"Let's do this right now," he said. "We don't have a lot of time," he said looking at us all. "One of you, clear the area where the puncture is. And one of you, fill this bucket with water while Joe and I sand the outside of the spot," Todd said giving us each roles to make this happen faster.

"Area's clear," Booger shouted.

"K, start sanding it, inside, all around the hole," Todd shouted.

Sean started sanding, Dave was getting water, and Todd and I sanded and talked.

"This gonna work?" I asked Todd.

"Should," he said back.

"Thanks for helping, man," I said sincerely.

"No, I fucked up," he said.

"Nah man, you've helped so much. Really, it is what it is," I replied accompanied by a continuous scratchy scrubbing sound as we sanded the boat.

We high fived and clapped a bunch of fiber glass dust and coughed and laughed.

"You should wear a mask for this," he said.

I pulled out my bandana and tied it over my face but we were already done.

"Alright, how's it looking up there?" Todd shouted up to Booger and Sean who were smoking a bowl.

"All good," Sean yelled back still holding a hit.

I climbed up and checked.

"Yup, looks good," I said.

"K, I'm gonna start mixing the fiberglass resin and then it's all time sensitive from there," Todd said.

"What else should we do?" Dave said, finally returning with the water bucket.

"Nothing, just chill and smoke. I'll fix this," Todd said and he went to work mixing and filling in the hole and it really didn't take him long, was only about an hour later, "Done," he said, obviously proud of his work.

"Are you serious?" Booger said.

"And I filled some other troublesome spots, like where the old propellor was," Todd said.

"Really? What the heck, Todd, dude? What were we worried about time for? You killed it," I said.

"It needs at least 24 hours to dry," he replied brining us back down to reality.

"Oh well, we should be good then right?" Booger asked.

"You'll need every minute and even some UV lights to help it set up through the night," he said very seriously. "To get it ready for a voyage," he added.

"Shit," Booger said.

"I have UV lights, be right back," Todd said and he ran back up the driveway.

"Yo, this is crazy," Sean said.

"Yeah, I was thinking the same," Dave said.

Me and Booger looked at each other.

"It's gonna be fine," I said once again trying my best to invoke confidence when really I felt the same way.

"Hope so," Booger said almost mumbling under his breath.

It was dark now and we could see bright lights coming towards us. It looked more like a UFO than a car, but it sounded like someone running kicking gravel.

"Todd?" I yelled at the strange glowing object coming faster and closer. "That you?" I asked.

"Yup," Todd replied again out of breath but this time bearing the lights attached to an extension cord. "Got the lights! Let's set these up directed on the patch job, inside and out and be done for today," he said.

"You're the fucking man, Todd!" I said feeling good about it all now but I seemed to be the only enthusiastic one.

"Yeah, thanks, Todd," Dave said.

"Thanks, man," Sean said.

"Thanks," Booger said.

"Sorry again everyone," Todd said.

"It's all good, man, everything's fixed. Let's smoke!" I said.

"Well, we don't know til its done hardening and back in the water really," Todd said.

I could tell he was feeling really bad about it all and not just for the hole, but maybe because it was starting to cost him more than he had expected.

"You did it how it was supposed to be done, right?" I asked.

"Yeah," he said.

"Well, then, it's gonna be great! I trust you, Todd," I said. But who really knows if it would hold up. I was back to just going with the flow. If it was meant to be, it was meant to be.

"Come up and smoke before you go," I said to Todd, but he just said goodbye and left.

The boys and I smoked and talked about anything but the boat until we smoked ourselves sleepy. We all went to bed anxious to see how the wound had healed in the morning or if it had at all.

Day 7

As soon as the morning light hit my eyes, I woke up and hurried down to check Todd's craftsmanship. When I got there, I could see I wasn't the first.

"How's it looking?" I asked Booger who was thoroughly inspecting the work Todd did and had my guitar with him, so he could have been jamming or smoking.

"Looks alright I guess, I wouldn't really know," Booger replied.

"Let me see," I said going over to it and tapping with my knuckles... knock knock knock. It sounded hollow. "Damn, yeah that could be good!" I exclaimed smiling and jumped and punched the air. Booger was smiling.

"I think we're back on, bro," I said to him grabbing the guitar that was leaning against the boat and picked it up and lit the bowl, taking a large wake and bake hit from the guitar pipe then handed it to Booger.

"Play me something piratey mate," I said in my pirate voice.

"Eye captain," he said and we smoked and sang. Booger was a talented musician and classically trained on the guitar. If I said, "Play me dunt dunt dunt bahp bahp bahp," he'd do it with a flair and I could make up the words on the spot or often had them written as poems or songs in my phone. Me and Booger and Sean and Dave had been playing music together for years like I said. Dave played rhythm guitar and bass if needed, but acoustically, he played guitar. Booger could do the fancier more complicated stuff like solos and arpeggio sweeps. Sean played the djembe or bongo and I sang and played a little guitar or drum.

"Shave his belly with a rusty razor!" Sean came down singing with Dave. Our small celebratory wake and bake must have woke them up finally.

"Hey you make-a toomucha noise!" another voice came yelling. It was Vinnie frantically waving his arms telling us to stop jamming. "Hey, you can'ta do thatta here."

We finally heard his strange American Italian accent and stopped, but it was too late, he looked pissed off.

"Sorry Vinnie," I said.

"You smoke and drink and play loud music. This issa notta party," Vinnie said angrily, stomping his little fit and creating a mini dust storm for ants I'm sure.

I didn't want to upset anyone but we really weren't hurting anyone and there was no one around his boat junk yard. Maybe we just woke him up or something, but he really didn't like us from the beginning.

"Vinnie, I'm sorry, man, really we're not bad guys, we're just artists, so we're strange," I said.

The guys rallied behind me in weirdness.

"Artists? What kind of a artists?" he asked, not quite believing us.

"Musicians, poets, and I'm a glass artist," I replied.

"Glass artist?!" he said back with shock. His whole demeanor changed.

"Yeah, well, I make little glass things on the torch and I call it art," I said laughing but seriously.

"Yes! Yes!" he said, "My fatha was a glass artist as well!" Vinnie said to us. "I remember as a little boy watching him in his shop making all the little trinkets of glass," he added.

I wasn't sure if we were talking about the same thing but I wasn't going to argue. Vinnie had a new perspective on us and the tension was gone into thin air.

"Wow! That's wild," I said. "Here you wanna hit?" I said handing him the guitar that was also a pipe.

"No, I don'ta know howta play rockn'roll," he said.

"Ha ha no, you can smoke out of it, though, if you want. There you hit that and light this," I said pointing out the hidden modification to the guitar.

"Wow! Wow! Ha ha!" he laughed and said, "Okay maybe small one," signaling with his fingers.

I lit it for him and he took a big rip and let it out coughing hard. Sean, Dave, and Booger looked on in amazement as the tables turned before their eyes and another voice called out.

"Vinnie! Vinnie! What the heck man? You're getting high with these guys? You never smoke with me?!" Todd shouted coming down the driveway with what looked like buckets of paint.

"Oh, give him a break," I yelled jokingly while Vinnie was still coughing.

"They make-a me do it! They make-a me do it!" Vinnie cried also joking and everyone laughed.

"Oh alright then," Todd said, looking like he felt left out.

"Here take a hit brudda," I said to Todd.

He smiled and took the guitar and a big hit. I strummed the top chord sending vibrations through his brain.

"Ha ha! That's crazy," he laughed, letting his hit out.

"Did you guys check it?" he asked.

"Yeah man looks good," I said, and he tapped it the same way I did.

"Does sound good," Todd said.

"Gooda job, Todd," Vinnie said.

"They helped, too," Todd said.

"Nah man, you did the important parts," I said.

"Yeah, it looks great, Todd, thank you," Booger said.

"Well, it was kinda my fault so…" Todd said shrugging his shoulders. "It's the least I could do."

"Thank you," Sean and Dave added in.

"Let's get some paint on there and finish it up," Todd said, holding up the buckets.

"Ima gonna go back to werk," Vinnie said and waved his arm, turning and leaving probably pretty stoned. "You guyz can stay assa long assa you need," he yelled back.

We all looked at each other smiling, "Thank you!" We yelled back in unison.

"I'll take care of this painting for you, you guys can go jam over there until I'm done," Todd said pointing to a large wooden gazebo overlooking the creek and the docks. It was run down but beautiful in its own rustic kind of way. A perfect place to blaze and play.

"Awesome!" Sean said, obviously feeling the same way.

"Chaah," Dave said and we gathered the instruments and some herbs and went over to it.

There was a very old German man sitting there, unmoving like he was a fixture holding a mug and staring straight in the sun's direction.

"Hello, good morning," I said to the unmoving man.

He turned his head slowly in our direction and said, "Goot morning."

I knew he was German before he even said a word. It must have been the little hat with the feather or that giant mug with the intricate designs I subconsciously categorized as German.

"We were going to play some music, is that okay with you?" I asked the man.

"Mk," he said like he could care less.

"Cool thanks," I said and we sat down in the chairs that were there and jammed.

We played our original songs. We played some covers. It was like a concert for this one dude who seemed not to notice. Meanwhile, Todd was just finishing up laying down the clear coat of paint which meant it was almost done. He came over to the gazebo for a couple of hits and told us it just needed to dry a bit longer and we might have her back in the water by sundown.

The Gazebo Show was turning into a real party when Vinnie returned with some beer. Everyone was drinking, smoking, having a good time, so we didn't get the boat in the water that night, but probably better off so the paint layers could dry better. Instead we spent another night "on the hard" as they would say, our boat still a fish out of water and although spirits were high, I couldn't help but think when would we get this bitch on the sea.

I didn't sleep much though, tossing and turning anxiously awaiting the light of the sun so we could get her back in the water and start our adventures. At one point I got up and hit the pipe and killed some roaches, cockroaches that were crawling around. They seemed to be getting worse after we loaded her up with some food and snacks which makes sense. I kind of felt bad killing all these roaches, but it was kill or be killed. I didn't want the boys or I to be eaten alive in our sleep by a swarm of roaches.

Thankfully Dave packed an airsoft pistol that shoots little plastic pellets so that's how I was getting them. Eventually, I fell back asleep.

Day 8

As soon as I closed my eyes the sun was on the rise and the orange glow made a bead of sweat drip down my crusty neck. I hadn't showered in days but it felt like weeks.

"Wake up boys, come on," I called out to the crew. "Come on boys, wake up!" I repeated. I heard some moans and groans as they stretched off their hangovers and passed Booger the pipe. "Ready for some adventures?" I asked him.

"Ugh, I don't think I can handle anymore adventures," he replied, wiping the sleepy dust from his eyelids.

"I am!" Dave said.

"Yup, let's go," Sean said.

"Shut up, bro, it hasn't even started yet," I said jokingly, but it had no doubt been an up and down rollercoaster of vibes since we left Hoffendoer's dock.

"Let's go see if she's ready to get back in the water," I said and we all went outside to see how it all looked. We actually were having a hard time even finding the patched spot. "That's fucking crazy," I said.

"I can't even tell where the spot was," Dave said.

"Ha ha, wild!" Sean said.

"Hope it holds up," Booger said sourly but he was just saying what we all were thinking, I guess.

"It will, man, TRUST," I said and started running up to Vinnie's building which was his business and his home, I believe but I don't know. Thankfully, he was there though because it was early.

"Aye Joey! Joey Glassman!" he yelled out when he saw me running up the driveway.

"Ha ha Vinnie hey!" I yelled back joyfully. I actually go by the name Jipse glass but I didn't want to confuse or bore him with that.

"I lika you guyz music last night. Very good!" he said smiling.

"Thanks so much, man, it was fun times, and thank you for letting us stay here and helping us out, we really, really appreciate it. Can I ask you one more favor?" I said.

"Anything," he said. "Whatcha need? he asked.

"Can you put us back in the water today at some point?" I asked, squinching, hoping not to be a bother.

"Whyya leava so soon?" he asked. "You donta needa rush," he added insistently.

"We're ready to adventure and anxious to get started," I said.

"Of course, of course. Whenever you're ready," he said.

"We're ready," I said and with that we both headed back to the boat and made it happen with the help of the crew and of course Vinnie and his equipment. We were soon lowering our sailboat back into the water.

We were all on edge knowing that the boat's buoyancy was based on how good Todd did the job.

The boat was in. The straps were off and everyone cheered except me who ran in to see how the fiberglass was holding up. It was fine.

"Looking good, boys!" I yelled ecstatically.

"Thank you, Vinnie!" I added and the crew repeated, "Thank you, Vinnie!"

"Hey, what about me?" Todd came walking down the dock smiling.

"Todd, dude! Thank you so so much, man. None of this would be possible without you and obviously, you did a killer job on the patch. Thank you thank you," I said.

"Yeah dude, thank you," Booger said sincerely.

"Woo hoo! Let's go!" Dave shouted out.

"Go where. Are you guys taking off for real?" asked Todd.

"I don't know, I guess we're about ready," I said.

"No you're not," Todd said.

"What? Why don't you think so?" I asked.

"You don't even have a life raft yet," Todd said.

"Oh fuck," I said, the whole crew just watching our important back and forth convo.

"You guys can go back to my dock until you're ready," Todd said.

"I thought they didn't want us there at your work," I said.

"They just didn't want any part of fixing the boat. But you guys are good to go back," Todd said.

"Oh word?" Dave said.

"Awesome, thank you," Booger said.

I was just frozen. I didn't know what to do. I just wanted to get going. No more pit stops.

"Do we need a dinghy?" I asked.

"Yeah, you gotta have certain stuff or you get in trouble out there, either by the law or just stranded without one when you need it," Todd said and then asked, "What's the problem?"

"I just want to get out there," I replied, but I knew we needed to get back to Todd's and figure out the dinghy situation. "But you're right and I'm being hasty, thanks Todd," I said.

"No problem, bro, it's all good," Todd said sounding more chill now that the boat was fixed and things seemed good.

He hopped in and checked out his handiwork and then said, "Cool, well let's go, oh, and I got something for you."

We said thanks again and goodbye to Vinnie and the unmoving man who was still in the same spot in the gazebo.

We started the engine and we were off, back to Todd's dock. Five minutes later and we were pulling up to Todd's spot, met by the strange sight of a full-grown man lounging in an inflatable boat on the dock, full of water, like a kiddy pool. It was Gill and he was awkwardly sporting his signature Speedo and sunglasses look.

"Come on in! The water's fine!" he laughed in a pirate's voice, splashing and drinking his beer, then spitting some out like a fountain.

"What the actual fuck, Gill?" I said laughing out loud as we tied up to the dock slowly.

"I'm kidding boys! I'm checking her for holes. Making sure she's solid. This be your new dinghy!" he continued in the pirate voice smiling.

"Oh shit! Dude!" I exclaimed.

"Yes!" the crew celebrated with cheering and fist bumps.

Gill just sat there smiling and raised his beer.

"Cheers!" he said.

"Aye," I said and I grabbed a pipe and ripped it.

"What else do we even need?" asked Booger.

"This," Todd interjected standing on his boat, holding something up, "A solar panel to recharge the battery and run the pump."

"Dude, you've given us so much, I can't take one more thing," I said.

"You need this," Todd said.

We had been so blessed by these people, so hooked up, it couldn't have been any better. I looked at Booger, "We're all set now, Booger. I say we set sail tomorrow," I declared.

"Tomorrow?" Todd asked, shocked.

"You guys really think you're ready," Gill asked.

"Ready as we'll ever be honestly," I replied.

I was waiting for the cheer of the crew again, but nothing came.

"Are we though?" Booger asked.

Sean and Dave now retired back into the cabin to roll a blunt.

"Yeah man we are. We'll go out. We'll stay close to shore. And if anything happens we can just motor in if we need to. Let's fill up on gas and go!" I said hitting my fist on the boat.

Dave stuck his head out and, "Down!" he said and I could hear Sean shout, "Down!" as he finished rolling.

"What are we waiting for, Booger?" I asked him.

"Wanna go for a tester?" Gill asked.

"No," I responded quickly but I could tell Booger thought otherwise.

"Why?" Gill asked.

"Yeah, why?" Booger asked.

"'Cause I don't want anything else to happen to the boat. It's finally good to go and I am worried we will fuck it up just taking it out for a joy ride," I said emphatically.

"Well, if something's going to happen, you want it to happen here," Gill said.

He was right but I hated the idea. I had the worst feeling about it, but the guys actually seemed excited and I felt like I didn't need the practice, but maybe they did.

"You're right," I said. "I just can't bear to see another thing go wrong, but yeah, better off now during the practice run rather than the real thing," I said to Gill.

"It'll be fine," Gill said.

"So, shall I save this for out there?" Sean said, brandishing the blunt he had just perfectly rolled.

"Yup," I said to Sean. "Prepare for a test run then, boys!" I yelled in a pirate voice.

"You're doing this?" Todd asked.

"Yeah, why?" I said to him.

"I was thinking what you were thinking about not breaking anything else," Todd said, getting off the boat shaking his head.

"Well, yeah, but it would suck if something happened at sea and we were screwed," I said.

"Be careful," he said, "See you when you get back."

"You're not coming?" I asked.

"Work," he replied and headed into the boat yard.

"Alright, well let's do this," I said, clapping my hands together.

"You ready?" Gill asked.

I looked at the crew and by the looks of their faces I could tell this is what they wanted.

"Let's do it," I said, and Gill hopped on board with me, Sean, Dave, and Booger.

I started our engine for another mini-journey, not the main journey, but a journey.

They had never been sailing so it would be all new to them. And I was glad we had Gill, who was very experienced to help out. We cruised slowly through the canal on our way out to the Bay, everyone taking a different position on the boat. Sean was on the bow looking out, Booger was on the roof of the cabin, holding onto the mast. Dave was inside smoking. And me and Gill sat around the captain's wheel on the bench seats.

"What's her name?" he asked.

"Her name?" I repeated.

"It's bad luck to not name your vessel, especially before a voyage," he said.

"Had no idea," I said, trying to listen and pay attention to where I was going.

We were coming out of the canal now and the little creek began to open out to the massive Bay that was like an ocean of its own.

Gill stood up on the bench and held on to one of the support wires for the mast and started barking orders at everyone, "Prepare the main sail!" he yelled at Booger who looked like he had just gotten in trouble. "Untie the cover quickly and be careful, it's like tissue paper!" he blasted through the wind that increased as we entered the Bay.

Booger started to untie the sail cover but he was taking his time. Enough time for Gill to run up there and do it ahead of him.

"Like this!" he pulled a string on each tie that quickly released the cover. "You've gotta be quick out here!" he said to Booger who now looked like he could cry, "You'll learn," Gill said.

"Yeah," Booger said, wiping his nose.

"You'd better or you'll all die," Gill said back yelling into the wind, his voice fading as he approached Sean daydreaming on the bow and shook him from his shoulders.

"Woah shit!" Sean said.

"Always hold on tight, Boyo! Ye don't want to fall off in the night," he said eerily. "Now go down and grab the front sail," Gill added.

"Which one's that?" Sean said.

"Figure it out," Gill said.

Sean just looked at him, "Go, now," Gill hurried him along.

Dave had just come out to join me at the helm, "Ready to spark this?" he said, still hanging on to the blunt when Gill came stomping back to us.

"Go help your mate find the right sail, it will either be the biggest or the smallest bag," Gill said to Dave.

Dave looked at me to confirm the orders.

"Yeah, we'll smoke that when we get going," I said and sent him back down into the cabin with Sean.

"Why you being so tough on them, man?" I turned to Gill who had a wild look in his eye.

"They need to learn," he said.

"Well, I don't wanna scare them out of it," I said.

"There's no room for mistakes out there," he said.

"I get it, man, but" I started, but he cut me off.

"There's no second chances out there," he said.

A life lesson I would learn to live my life by.

Just then, Sean and Dave came out.

"Got it!" Sean yelled.

"I found it though," Dave said laughing.

"Good, go attach it," Gill said.

"How do we do that?" Sean asked holding the giant sail bag with the sail in it.

"Ya find the top of the sail and clip it to the top clip and so on," Gill replied flatly.

"Alright, we'll give it a shot," Dave said.

"No you'll fucking do it," Gill said.

"Geesh, man, we'll try our best," Sean said kind of but not really laughing.

"There is no try, there is only do," Gill said.

"He's trying to teach us the hard way," I said.

"The right way," Gill said.

"Well take it easy. Booger's gonna cry," I said, kind of joking as well, trying to lighten the mood, but it back fired.

"No I'm not," Booger cried.

"I know, I'm just joking," I said to Booger who was still holding down the uncovered main sail, while Dave and Sean worked together to get the front sail attached.

"How's it coming?" I yelled up to them.

"Almost," Dave said.

"Nope, try again," Gill yelled.

"What?" Sean yelled.

"You've got it upside down," Gill replied and they began undoing it and trying again.

We were pretty far out in the bay now, with no other boats around. I could have stopped and made it easier for all this to be done, but I could see Gill was trying to recreate a real life scenario with winds and pressure so I kept the engine going and we kept moving.

"Think it's good," Dave yelled.

"Alright, raise the sails then," Gill yelled.

They looked confused.

"The ropes on the mast," I yelled.

Booger reached for the rope on the mast nearest him and started pulling it down and it began hoisting the main sail up. With every pull of the rope, the large off white tissue paper material sail unfolded, making a scary crunchy crinkling noise, which made it clear how fragile this important piece was.

"Slow and steady," Gill said.

Dave grabbed the other line on the other side of the mast and began hoisting the front sail. It was looking good. We were looking like sailors. I killed the engine and turned the boat to catch some wind. The sails puffed up, inflated with the bay breeze and the lines creaked as they tightened. Everything tightened up and the boat heeled over, leaning hard on her side.

"Whooooah!" Sean let out a wild yell as he hung on the bow sprint for dear life.

"Ha ha!" I laughed out.

"Fuck no!" Booger jumped down by me.

"Yo! Sean almost fell off!" Dave screamed.

"Hang on tight," Gill yelled.

We were fucking sailing and I was genuinely glad we did this practice run as the boat crashed through the waves.

"Take the helm!" I yelled at Booger who looked scared out of his mind.

"Wha? Okay," he said grabbing the wheel.

"Keep her straight!" I said as I threw a long rope that was tied to the boat off into the water.

"What are you doing?" Gill asked.

"You'll see, I said, going down into the cabin and grabbing my surfboard. I took it and jumped off the boat and found the rope in the water and climbed onto my board. I was being dragged behind the boat on my board. It was like a 100 foot rope, so I don't know what they were doing but I was just having fun. I put the rope in my teeth and held on while I popped up on my board and surfed the little wake we were making from our sailboat. It felt like a once in a lifetime opportunity I wanted to take advantage of, so I did for a few minutes and then reeled myself back in. I returned to see the crew was holding up fine without me which was a good feeling to know they had a better idea of how it all worked.

"Ready to smoke?" I yelled grabbing a towel and drying off.

"Yup!" Sean shouted back.

"Alright, lower the sails," I yelled and so it was done.

My motley crew were now sailors.

"Let's get that main sail folded and covered back up nice," I said to Booger. He seemed to be the right person for that job which required a bit more responsibility and attention to detail.

"Eye eye captain," Booger said.

"Unclip that sail and put her away," I said to Sean and Dave, pointing to the front sail. "And bring me that blunt!" I added.

"Eye eye captain!" Sean exclaimed.

"Thanks, Gill," I said to Gill who also looked pleased.

"You're ready now," Gill said smiling.

Sean handed me the blunt. I smiled back, lit it up and started the engine as I took us back into shore. The sun was going down as we pulled up to Todd's dock with the blunt still burning. Gill jumped off and onto the dock as soon as we were close enough and began tying the boat down.

"Who's hungry?" Gill shouted already heading towards his ship.

"I am," I shouted back and then looked at the guys. "We are," I shouted again, answering for the crew. They were beat, they looked like zombies, stoned zombies. We had worked them pretty hard. "You guys good?" I asked.

"Yeah."

"Eh."

"Ya."

A mixture of groaning, mumbles, I'm not sure from who, but I got the point.

"Hey, you're gonna love this. Gill's a great cook. I think he went to school for it or something."

The news brought life back to the zombie crew and they all perked up with excitement. We looked over to see Gill coming off his ship. He had a watermelon under one arm and a tied up grocery bag in his hand and a cooler in the other.

"What's for dinner?" I yelled over to him.

"Steak, lobster, watermelon and beer for dessert," he yelled back setting it down around his mini-grill still on the dock from previous cookouts. I felt the jaws drop around me and checked left and right to see.

"Ya hear that?" I asked.

"He's joking right?" Booger asked.

"Yeah that's code word for sardines," I said laughing. "No, yeah, it's real and he's like a fucking master chef," I added still laughing.

"For real?" Dave said.

"Yes dudes!" I laughed out.

"I'm gunna fucking destroy that shit," Sean said in a muffled filtered voice with a mouthful of smoke, squishing the blunt roach out in the sink that didn't work and with a very serious look on his face.

We all laughed.

Todd must have seen us pull up because he came walking over, looking glad to see us back in one piece.

"How was it?" he asked.

"Awesome!" Booger said pretty enthusiastically. He had really come a long way since this all started, a full 180 really, he was like a different dude.

Me, Sean and Dave looked at him surprised of his response.

"Yeah it was," Dave said.

"Mhm," Sean said, "Wild!" he added looking distracted by the thought and smell of delicious gourmet food merely steps away from his animalistic senses.

"Yeah, they learned how to sail today, man. I think we're ready," I said to Todd who was still standing on the dock listening but also looking over at Gill cooking.

"Good, gotta know how to sail if you want to go on a voyage," Todd said stating the obvious.'

"Yup," I said climbing off the boat.

"Alright, come grab a piece," Gill shouted standing over the flickering flames of the mini grill, holding a spatula and a piece of something he was eating.

"Nice!" Sean burst and was there in the blink of an eye.

"Wooo!," Dave and Booger and I cheered.

"You can have some, too," Gill said to Todd.

"Nah, I ate already," Todd said. "But I'll hang out," he added.

"This is delicious, Gill," Booger said, already devouring whatever he had in his hand.

"Is that the steak or lobster?" Gill asked.

"Steak," Booger said.

"Here try this," Gill said.

"Oh my duuude," Booger said as he savored the flavor of a piece of lobster made by pirate chef Gill.

"Let me try that," Dave grabbed a piece, "Fuck, Bro, that's crazy good,"

"Ha ha," I laughed stuffing some in my face. "Told you," I said.

"You were right, man," Sean said, lost in the food.

"Thank you so much, Gill, this is amazing, and Todd, dude for everything. Shit, both of you for everything. I could never repay you honestly," I said sincerely.

"Play us some tunes and get me high for starters," Gill said smiling and winked.

"Deal," I said.

"You know what to do boys," I said to Sean, Dave and Booger.

They went and grabbed the instruments and we played and got stoney and drank late into the night eventually falling asleep somewhere under the stars.

Everyone had a good time, but we all knew our crew would be departing soon, and no one said anything about it. I think they were going to miss us and I know I at least was going to miss them. We did talk about one thing I remember, the name of the boat again came into question.

"Did ya think of a name?" Gill asked.

"Seaweed smoker," Sean said.

"Ha ha," we laughed.

"That might be too obvious," Gill said.

"Pipe dreams?" I said.

"Ooh, I like that," Dave said.

"Still too obvious," Gill said sternly, "You don't want to bring any unwanted attention out there.

"True," I said. "Umm," I thought out loud.

"FREE," Booger yelled and we paused, "'Cause that's how I felt out there today," he said.

"Can we do that?" Dave asked?

"Sure," Gill said.

"What if someone thinks the boat is free and they take it?" Sean asked.

"Then they're an idiot who should be locked up," Gill said.

"I like it, man, you guys down?" I said to Sean and Dave.

"Yeah."

"For sure," they said.

"Then it's official. And we cheersed, pipes and bottles."

Day 9

When they woke up the next morning, I was already making it official and painting the name on our vessel.

"F-R-E-E" it spelled out in big, black, capital letters with the quotes to dissuade any would-be boat thieves.

"Killed it," Sean said.

I hadn't even heard anyone get up so I was shocked to find them all around me, looking at the work I had just done.

"Hey! Ha ha! You like?" I asked the crew.

"Yeah, looks great," Dave said smiling.

"That is perfect," Booger exclaimed.

I tried to make it look fancy, but it obviously wasn't professionally done, which I thought added character.

"Where'd you get the paint?" Booger asked.

"Todd found some extra at work. He said we could use or keep and he said goodbye and nice meeting you in case he doesn't catch us before we go," I said. "But he's gonna try and pop back over soon," I added.

"Go?" Booger said completely ignoring the paint part.

"Yeah, I thought we were leaving today?" I said.

"Guess I kinda forgot," Booger said nervously looking around at the others.

"I'm ready," Dave said shrugging.

"I've been ready," Sean said eagerly.

Smash! The sound of shattering exploding as I broke a glass bottle over the edge of the boat.

"Then I christen the 'The Free!'" and poured some rum down my throat letting out a howl of sorts. "WooOO!"

And the crew cheered as we passed the broken bottle around.

"So when do we leave?" Booger asked.

"Let's get ready to go and when we are all set if it feels right, we leave," I said.

"Today?" Booger said.

"Yes," I said. "Today."

More cheers from Sean and Dave, now packing pipes and rolling joints.

"That's good preparation, men, but let's also check the safety equipment, like the flares, radio, dinghy, etcetera; check the gas, water, food reserves, stuff like that," I said and we got to it.

Now I didn't really drink much, but it felt like the pirate thing to do. It was the christening of our boat and celebration of our maiden voyage. Plus, I was getting tired of hose water from the dock.

"Good! You're still here!" Todd said excited walking up on us but everyone kept busy checking the boat.

"Not fer long," I said proudly one foot up on the edge of the boat.

"You guys really going?" Todd asked.

"Of course we're going. What do ya think we are?" I asked. "Landlubbers!" I added in a pirate accent.

"Yarrgh!" Sean yelled like a pirate as well.

"Oh okay," Todd laughed at us. "Are you drunk?" he asked me.

"No," I said. "Are you?" the pirate accent continued and it didn't stop 'til much much later.

"Ha ha, okay Joe, be careful," Todd said.

"Ha ha, okay yar. We just christened our vessel and now we are preparing to set sail." I shouted.

The commotion finally interested Gill enough who was standing on the bow of his ship, which was lined up with the rear of our ship, so he could see the fresh paint.

"Ooh ""The Free"," Gill said. "Look's good, mate," he said, stretching off another hangover.

"Oh let me see," Todd said, leaning over the water to catch a look at the new name on the back of the boat.

"That'll work," he said laughing. "Actually, I gotta get back to work, but I'm glad I got to say goodbye, in case you guys really leave today," Todd said looking kind of sad.

"It's not forever, Todd, we'll see you again someday. Thank you for everything," I said and I jumped off the boat and high five one-arm hugged him, then got back on my boat.

The boys yelled their goodbyes and Todd was gone.

"Today the day then?" Gill shouted.

"Tis indeed," I yelled back.

"Eye," he said. "Make sure you've got everything you need," he said.

"Eye," I said back continuing to ready the ship while drinking rum, smoking weed, and eating the most convenient thing I could find, some chocolate covered pomegranate things, no doubt something Booger packed.

Before we knew it, we were all sitting around the helm, smoking with Gill like it was another day.

"Wait, are we goin' or what?" I said standing up on the seat holding on to a wire above my head for stability.

"Ready when you are, Captain," Sean said.

"I don't know, are we really doing this?" Booger asked, the only one not in pirate voice.

"Yes, mate, but ye don't have to come with us," I said.

"No, I want to," Booger said.

"You can always come back," Gill said and it eased all of our tensions especially Booger's who smiled.

"Yeah that's true," Booger said clearly feeling much better about leaving for a journey on a sailboat at sea with little to no experience of ever sailing in search of a mythical island covered in weed led by a teenage modern day caveman who thinks he's a pirate.

"Eye, it is, but we won't be coming back," I said eerily.

"Untie that line," I said as I started the engine and pointed to the rope near Sean.

Gill jumped out of the sailboat and onto the dock and saluted us.

"May the wind always be at yer back," he said and waved as I started to pull away steering us down the canal.

"Thanks for everything!" I yelled.

"Bye," the crew yelled over the engine.

Was this really happening, I was thinking. I wasn't thinking though. I was just going for it. Balls to the wall. All or nothing.

The canal opened into the bay and I put the pedal to the medal full throttle which was still pretty slow, but faster than we'd been going when that free feeling kicked in for all of us at the same time, the boat erupted in cheering from everyone.

"This is awesome!" Dave said.

"Crazy," Sean said.

"When should we put up the sails?" Booger asked.

"Let's wait 'til we're past the bridge," I said.

"Why?" Booger asked.

"Because I just want to get out there and not fiddle with sails in the Bay, and don't question me, mate. There's gonna be a lotta things I say that need to be done without question from here on out. That goes for all of ya," I said.

"Okay," Booger and the boys said like soldiers, realizing I was serious, and maybe seriously drunk too.

It really wasn't until we hit the open water that I started to feel it. We had just gone under the massive bridge and gotten the farthest out that we had all traveled when the water very suddenly changed from calm little ripples to an angry, aggressive, abrasive ocean tossing our little boat while the poor excuse for an engine screamed horribly as it plunged in and out of the water. Vrooom! Vrooom! Vrooom! All types of noises and it was then the alcohol hit me. I was wasted like I had never been before.

"Prepare the sails!" I yelled as I continued throttling us into waves. I was worried if I stopped they'd just splash into the boat anyway and sink us.

The crew looked at me frozen like a deer in headlights.

"Should we go back?!" Booger yelled.

"Prepare the sails!" I yelled and they jumped to it.

Sean and Dave grabbed the front sail from the storage room bathroom while Booger untied and uncovered the main sail.

They were doing great but I was not, I felt so sick and I couldn't tell if I was sea sick or if it was from drinking and eating junk all day, either way I was in bad shape, but I just wanted to keep going. I knew if we could get the sails set, I could take a little rest and sleep it off. We'd be on our way to Sensemilla Island.

"Is this right?" Dave yelled out from the bow as it bobbed 6 plus feet in the air over and over again. Just watching him and Sean going up and down from the back was making me sicker and increasingly worried that we might not get the sails set before I lose it.

"Upside down!" I yelled back, but it was no easy task, they had to unclip and tie it all in the blowing wind and bouncing waves and it was obvious they were struggling.

"Come take the helm!" I shouted and Dave came back to the wheel, hanging on for dear life the whole way. I stomped up to the bow in frustration of my inebriation pretending the chaos wasn't there. I just wanted to set this sail correctly so we could be on our way and I could puke and pass out.

"Ahoy!" Sean greeted me yelling through the wind but I was in a drunken fog with only the smallest window of focus energy and it was needed for this sail. I grabbed the sail from him and laid on my back on the bow. We were already practically sitting trying to stay on the boat and keep from being tossed off.

Figuring out miraculously which was top and what was bottom, I started clipping the sail to its line and Sean helped. We were standing now and he grabbed the rope to hoist it.

"Okay," I yelled. "Raise the sails."

Sean began raising the front and Booger started raising the main while Dave was still at the wheel. I stumbled back towards Dave and took his place.

"Ya okay?" he asked.

"Yup," I yelled.

"You don't look so good man," Dave said.

"Let's just get her all set to go," I said. "And then I might yack or something," I added.

He looked at me not sure what to say.

"Shit!" Booger yelled as he tied the line and jumped back towards us followed by Sean.

The sails were up now, all I had to do was angle them to catch wind and let one of the boys take over. I pulled the lines hard and the wind fought back forcing the boat to lean hard. We had a beautiful breeze right on our backs and I tied the lines in place as the crew held on and watched.

"There," I said. "All set. Dave, take the helm. I'm going to throw up now."

And I proceeded to get very, very sick for about half an hour or more until retiring to the cabin with no idea of where we would end up.

Day 9 ½

When I finally did wake up I could hear the soothing sounds of rolling waves and see the sun was shining bright. It was like a brand new day as I stepped out from the cabin. I could see Dave still sitting there at the helm smiling. And I was pretty sure we were going to be heading home, but to my surprise, there was no land in sight, which startled me a bit.

"Where are we?" I asked back in my normal voice staring out at the vast openness of the Gulf and sounding like someone who just woke up from a drunken stupor.

"We be at sea!" Dave said in his pirate voice.

"How far at sea?" I replied. We hadn't turned around and in fact were further out than I'd expected we'd even go.

"Bout thirty miles off shore GPS says," Booger replied in his best pirate voice. It needed some work. But they were doing great and enjoying themselves.

"How was yer nap, Captain?" Sean asked laughing.

"Hey, hey, hey," I said. "That was a test. Wanted to see if you boys could handle it without me before we got too far on the journey in case anything were to happen to me. And you passed with flying colors!" I said creating an almost believable excuse for my embarrassing actions.

"Uh huh," Dave said smirking in disbelief.

"What's our heading?" I barked out back in pirate voice.

"West, Southwest," Booger shouted out.

"Good man, Booger," I said acknowledging his quick directional skills. "Let's change it to straight South," I said, "Swap spots with me," I said to Dave and switching seats with Dave began turning our ship in a new direction.

I figured we had gone out far enough and it was time to head in the Island's direction now.

"Adjust the sails," I yelled to the crew who got right to work and we were off again, catching more wind that almost seemed to change direction with us.

"Sensemilla Island here we come!" I yelled and we all cheered, "I need to rest more so I can sail through the night," I said so I could go smoke a bowl and lay down to try to feel better. I was still having residual stomach aches and just felt kinda shitty from the puking and heaving, but in saying this to them I was just understanding what needed to be done too, like we were all finding out at the same time.

"Through the night?" Booger asked.

"Well we can't stop in the middle of the sea and sleep, the anchor's not long enough. We'd end up in China," I said.

"What about going back to shore?" Dave said.

"You want to?" I asked him.

"Not really," he said.

"Yeah and it would add so much time to the trip," I said.

"So straight there!?" Sean asked excitedly.

"Yup," I said smiling and heading back into the cabin for another nap. "Just keep this heading. Wake me if you need me!" I said and I went in and sat on a bench, hit the pipe and laid down, instantly falling asleep.

"Joe, Joe!" Booger was whisper yelling, shaking me, trying to wake me up. "What should we do?"

I heard him calling deep from dreamland and remembered I was on a treasure hunt in real life and my crew needed me. I woke up and jumped to my feet with fresh life. I could see Sean was asleep there on the triangle bed, which meant he was going to be my other crewmate staying up with me sailing through the night.

"We should switch positions and continue on," I yelled.

It was dusk now and I understood why they were worried. We were heading into the unknown and the captain was completely useless until now.

"We weren't sure if we should head in towards land or what?" Booger said, "You seemed pretty fucked up."

"I'm good. I'm good," I said trying to reassure him and whoever else could hear that we were fine. "How's things been?" I asked not even sure if that came out right.

"Been good," Booger said to me as I headed out onto the deck.

"Eye Captain," Dave yelled.

"How ya been?" I asked Dave.

"Smooth sailing," he said happily.

"Well good, you ready to switch with us?" I asked Dave and Booger.

"Sure," Booger said.

"Eh, I'm good. I'll go 'til the sun goes down," Dave said.

"Alright perfect, gives me time to eat and smoke," I said trying to assess the situation and to understand fully what I had to do next.

"Sean, boyo!" I said, sounding like a pirate, "Wake up, mate," I said giving his foot a shake with my hand. "It's pirate time! It's our turn," I said with a grin.

He lifted his head, looked at me and said, "Holy Fuck I thought this was a dream," and then burst out laughing.

"It is mate, a dream come true. Now come get ready with me for our shift," I said, holding up the pipe Todd let us keep and a cold pot of rice the boys must have cooked up earlier.

"Yes sir!" he laughed. "Hey, how ya feeling?" he asked.

"Feeling good and soon much better," I said taking a hit from the pipe.

"Cheers!" Sean said quickly.

"Cheers!" I said with a mouthful of smoke handing him the pipe.

"Smells good down there!" Dave yelled from the helm.

"Want a hit?" I yelled back.

"Nope, I'll be down there soon," he said sounding tired.

"Right O," I yelled back, knowing it was our turn soon and shoved more rice in my face. "Want some?" I asked Sean.

"Ate earlier man thanks," he said starting to smoke while we were bounced around in the cabin.

It wasn't exactly smooth sailing but we were moving right along with no problems so it was going smoothly.

We still had the wind at our backs pushing us right to our destination or so we believed. I was beginning to wonder how far we had gone but tried to put that out of my mind because it was anyone's guess plus we figured heading straight south from where we started we should run right into the islands, so why worry.

"Okay, I'm done," Booger yelled from outside.

"Ready to switch," Dave yelled and me and Sean looked at each other, shared another couple quick pipe hits, and climbed out of the cabin.

The antique yellow glow lighting the interior of the cabin tricked my senses into blindness as I stepped out into the pitch black night.

"Holy shit how could you guys see anything?" I asked.

"We can't, that's why we're switching," Booger said, laughing as he went into the cabin and passed me quickly.

"No stress, I'm sure our eyes will adjust," I said grabbing the wheel from Dave.

"Yeah you'll be fine," Dave said as he got up from his seat. I could tell he looked beat so my eyes must have started to adjust already.

"Good job keeping us alive," I said to Dave, slapping him on the back as he went down into the cabin.

"Thanks," he said back as he plopped onto the nearest bench, that was not being affected negatively by the angle of the boat. With the ship being heeled over at an angle one bench was always compromised by gravity forcing the person on it to roll right off.

"Sean, get to the bow and let me know if we are about to hit anything," I yelled out to Sean who was already there.

"Eye eye," he yelled from the front.

We had a nice night breeze blowing us directly south. The water was choppy but not crazy. I could see the bits of moonlight reflecting off every peak of every little wave around us, shimmering like twinkling stars. There were no lights from the cities and no sign of life at all out there. Just the moon, the stars, and us as we continued sailing like it was really nothing new to us. I sat down at the helm and grabbed the wheel with one hand looking out at the mysterious world I was traveling through in real life. I had only dreamed of this or seen it in movies until now and here I was with my crew in our boat "FREE". The sails were set and only ever needed slight adjustments of tightening or letting them out and I suddenly found myself amazed that I actually felt bored and or anxious knowing I had to just sit here, holding this position for the next 12 hours only to get up to use the bathroom everything else could be done from here and honestly you just pee off the back, mostly.

"Let me get that pipe when you're done with it," I called down to Dave and Booger.

"K," Booger yelled back. "Actually, here," he came out and brought me the pipe and the whole bag of weed." I'm passing out now and Dave's already out," he said.

"Nice thank you," I said. "Good job today," I added as he went back down.

"Thanks man, night," he said back.

"Night Booger," I said, ready to do my shift now that I had the pipe and tree.

The weed was in a diving gear bag that was emptied and weighted with weights we cut from our bait casting net, so if we got pulled over by the Coast Guard we could just dump it in the ocean and let it sink. We heard some crazy stories before we left about sailors getting caught with weed and getting their boats taken and sent to jail. We knew what we were risking, but it was part of the fun.

"See anything?" I called up to Sean.

"Nope," Sean replied.

"Well come on back here and hit this with me," I shouted and he came jumping back towards me excited.

"Nice!" he said sitting down next to me on the side bench by the wheel.

"Here, pack it and spark it," I said passing him the pipe and bag of weed.

It was hard to pack and light in the wind and darkness and all of the motion of the ocean.

"On it," he said and went into the cabin where he packed a fresh bowl and sparked it up to get it cherried. "Ear," he came out hastily with the burning pipe barely able to speak from his fat hit.

"Oh nice thank you!" I said quickly grabbing the piece and ripped it and passed it back fast to keep it going.

"Cheers," I said.

"Cheers," he said.

We smoked and laughed cruising in our vessel steady through the night, all alone out there, not a soul for miles. I started getting tripped out, lost in thought. What if a giant sea monster whale just jumps up and swallows our little boat whole? It was suddenly crazy to me how far we were from reality and civilization. The possibility of anything happening amplified the feeling of freedom, not knowing what might happen next.

"Right, I'm gonna go back up front and see if anything is happening," Sean said.

"Alrightee!" I said in a stoney pirate voice sitting back and looking at the stars and the moon I became aware my eyes had fully adjusted and I could now see the night life of the ocean clear as day.

I smiled high as I steered our ship and thought of what we had accomplished to get here. I noticed the moon and stars were moving because I was aimed at the moon and heading south, but when I tried to use the moon as a reference point again I began heading southwest. I could see on the compass attached to the helm some hours must have gone by and I could feel my eyelids getting heavy.

"You good up there?" I yelled to Sean thinking if I was getting tired, he must be, too.

"Yeah," he said sounding like he just woke up.

"Go down and get some shut eye in the cabin. I'll wake you if I need you," I told him, the last thing we needed was to lose a mate overboard I thought, imagining him falling asleep and rolling off the bow in the night. I wouldn't know until it was too late.

"Nah, I'm good," he said.

"There's nothing out there, man. It's all good," I said trying to reassure him and myself.

"You sure?" he asked.

"Yeah man it's fine. I'll holler if I need something, actually will you pack that pipe for me first?" I said.

"Word, ya, for sure. Should I spark it too?" he asked.

"Nah, not unless you need a hit," I said.

"Nah, I'm good," Sean replied and went into the cabin and packed me a bowl and then gave it back to me. "Night bro, I'll be ready if you need me," he said.

"Thank you so much brother, good night. I should be fine," I said and with that he retired to the cabin for some much, much needed sleep.

We had been traveling on a nonstop voyage and it was our first ever. I started thinking of the friends we met that hooked us up: Ty, Todd, Gill, and Vinnie while I sat sailing our beautiful vessel only made possible by the most random chance encounters. Then I thought of Mr. Hoffendoer, the guy we got the boat off of. He was sending us to our deaths and did not give one fuck. He just collected his money and sent us off sailing for the islands in a busted boat. We wouldn't have made it far on just a battery without the solar panel from Todd to recharge the battery that ran the pump that drained any leakage from the center board or old propellor spot. It would have died and the boat would have filled with water and who knows what. Getting lost in thought, I started to doze off but quickly caught myself.

"That could be dangerous," I laughed at myself and tried lighting the lighter to hit the pipe but it was almost impossible with wind blowing lightly from all directions it felt like, but it was still from directly behind us. So I figured why not just crouch down low next to the wheel blocked by the benches and the side of the boat and light it. I got down low and was sitting on the floor of the deck between the helm and the bench and began to smoke. It was working and I could still steer from down there. I knew it was dangerous, but I couldn't see in front of me to begin with. I was determined to keep this ship moving in the right direction and stay awake doing it alone through the night but it didn't happen.

I fell asleep, I'm not sure for how long, but long enough to scare me. I could have killed us. We could have crashed or randomly capsized while we all slept. That reality woke me up in a different kind of way which kept me sailing steady till the moon went down and light emerged on the horizon and for a moment half the sky was lit.

I had been waiting for that very moment anxiously, no later, no sooner, just that gorgeous first light.

Day 10

"BOYS!" I yelled, "BOYS! WAKE UP!"

"You good?!" Booger said sounding worried and poking his head out squinting at the approaching morning light.

"We're still alive aren't we?" I said.

"Uh, yeah," Booger said.

"Then I'm great," I said, "Come relieve me of my position," I said.

"K," he said popping back into the cabin and waking the boys.

"What the fuck are you doing down here?" I could hear Booger yelling at Sean.

"It's alright Boy O, I sent him down last night," I yelled down through the cabin doors and the crew all came out onto the deck.

"You wha?" Dave said.

"You could've killed us," Booger said.

I'd better not tell him what happened then, I thought as I laughed out loud, "It was all good, she's ""Unsinkable,"" remember?" I said, using air quotes. "I had it under control," I said, Booger and Dave still looking at me dumbfounded in disbelief.

"Don't do that man," Booger scolded me.

"You're right man, once we get our sleep schedule on track it will be easier but I didn't want Sean to fall asleep on the bow and roll into the ocean, we'd never find him, so tonight whoever is on watch should tie themselves to the boat somewhere for safety or just both people sit at the helm while one person checks on the front every once in a while," I said and they agreed.

"Cool," Dave said.

"Good plan," Booger added as he grabbed the wheel.

It was still dark with just the sign of sun in the distance, but it would be up fully soon. The wind, like magic kept its pace and we were still headed South, destined for Sensemilla Isle. I felt confident handing over the reins as I stumbled down into the cabin without a word and crashed on a bench.

"How much longer ya think till we get there?" I heard Dave as I started to drift off to dreamland and responded face down in the bench padding muffled, "Uh could be today," I said and I was gone.

I don't think too much time had passed though when I was awakened by the lack of movement the ship was making, and a delicious familiar smell of some stinky nuggets burning. Had we stopped? Was I dreaming? It felt like we were at the dock just rocking in place. I was still exhausted but had to get up and see what was going on.

"Ahoy Matees!" I said dramatically as I opened the cabin door to behold a very strange scene.

An eerie dreamy silvery haze surrounded us highlighted by the golden glow of the sun lost in the fog somewhere. The silver hue of the sky was met by its silver reflection in the sea and I couldn't tell where one started and the other one stopped. We were sailing through the hazy heavens, and the boys were just sitting there smoking tree as we bobbed lifelessly in a stagnant body of water.

"Hey," Dave said.

"Hey," Booger said.

"Yoo," Sean said, and I could tell the moral was low.

"What's happening?" I asked.

"No wind," Booger said looking a little funny with a big floppy hat and fingerless gloves on with a little white zinc patch on his nose.

"Oh alright, no problem," I said trying to bring some life back to the party, "We could motor if we want to get there faster or we can chill and jam?" I said making a face and motioning my hands persuasively.

"Jam?" Booger asked.

"I'm down to jam," Dave said.

"Yeah," Sean said.

"Yeah, let's just enjoy it, sittin' here in the middle of nowhere, smoking freely just bobbin on the sea," I said, "Let's make a new one about just that actually," I added.

"Nice," Dave said and they went and grabbed the instruments from the cabin while I took the helm and some fat wake and bake rips to try and catch up to their level.

They were stoney and disheveled from these couple days already and I bet we looked like a wild bunch of dudes. I think we were all more than a little tired, delirious, and anxious to hit land soon so this was a good break from it all. I was still so tired I wasn't sure if this was just a figment of my imagination as I sat smoking and floating in foggy infinite space. But when they came back on deck laughing and joking, carrying the instruments I knew this was real and it was probably once in a lifetime as I smiled at them and took another hit.

"What shall we play for yee Captain?" Booger asked and Sean and Dave continued laughing.

"I was just saying something about bobbing, I'm gonna go with that and you guys play along when you feel the beat," I said and they knew what to do. I started free-styling our new song of the sea and they filled it with harmonious rhythms and sounds of guitar and bongo, creating one of our most genuine sounding melodies we ever made and it went like this;

We're bobbin' on the ocean

We're bobbin' on the sea

We're Bobbin' like Marley

If you know what I mean

When you live on the ocean

Life is so easy

> When you live on the ocean
>
> You can live free
>
> We're bobbin on the ocean
>
> We're bobbin on the sea
>
> We're Bobbin' like Marley
>
> If you know what I mean
>
> Yeah You know what I mean

    We must have amazed ourselves, because as it came to an end 20 minutes later, we all cheered in excitement for our new song and also what it said in the song, and how we were living it. I took some more fat rips off the pipe smoking and smiling and passed it around.

    "Killed it brothers," I said blowing out my smoke.

    "Yeww!" Sean cheered.

    "That was sick," Dave said.

    "Yeah I like that one a lot guys, let's remember it," Booger said stating the obvious.

    "Nope, forgot it already," Sean said, just trying to be a dick.

    "Shut up, you know what I mean," Booger said.

    "Haha alright, you guys ready to get moving?" I asked.

    "Yeah," Dave said.

    "Engine time?" Sean asked.

    "Yup," I said as I quickly turned and leaned over the back to crank the motor when PLOP!

    "Fuck!" I yelled.

    "What!"

    "What!?" everyone yelled back.

I turned around and sat back down and sullenly said, "Dropped my phone."

"Fuuuck," they all said as I slouched back.

"Welp, that's that, nothing we can do," I said.

"Pinned it!" Sean said, as in he pinned the location of where we were in the ocean and where the phone had dropped.

"Nice now we'll always know where it is," I said getting up and making my way to the cabin, "I'm going back to bed, wake me when there's wind," and I went and passed out leaving them on a bobbing boat in a silver haze.

DAY 10 ½

When I woke back up it was almost sunset and we were no longer bobbing, it now felt instead solid like a rock. No wind no motor running, just the boys sitting around passing a pot of rice and beans mixed with some canned chicken, corn and mayo, (that was surprisingly good unrefridgerated), our new go-to meal, for as long as we had the resources.

"Working hard I see," I said laughing and stretching as I stepped out onto the deck and grabbed the pot from Booger, stuffing my face with whatever was left.

"Yeah not much going on out here," Dave said looking stoned, full, and tired of doing nothing.

"No wind," Sean said agreeing.

"All DAY!" said Booger grabbing the pot back to see if there was any left.

"Damn," I said disappointingly, "Let's get moving," and I started the engine.

We were trying to use as little gas as possible. We only brought so much, but we couldn't just sit there spinning in circles. We cruised with the engine on for about an hour. Sean and Dave went to sleep and it became dark again leaving me and Booger to man the ship. I thought that the wind I was feeling was only from using the engine and cruising but it was still there faintly when we stopped motoring. The light wind was perfect for our jib a big front sail we had. It was made for light wind like this specifically. I went and got the sail from the cabin and me and Booger set it up with ease and no eye adjustment problems. There was a full moon and it was like a spotlight on us and the water was our stage. It was so flat as soon as we hoisted the jib up it started catching wind and we started moving.

"Wooo!" I let out a sound.

"Whoah," Booger yelped.

"Hang on to that line, don't let it go!" I yelled at Booger as he tried tying the line down for the sail. If a line from a sail gets free, it will come undone and have to be thread like a needle but the needle is a mast and the eye is the top of it.

"Got it," he yelled back, we were really moving faster than expected. The water was like glass as we cut through it smashing its calm serenity with our sleek vessel, breaking the moon's reflection along the surface of the mirror-like ocean. Instead of choppy, slappinig water, we were gliding with ease. The only sound was a never-ending shhhhhhh as we moved cleanly through like a hot knife through butter, our ship melting the very sea beneath us. And then the boat started to turn and we lost our wind for a moment because no one was at the helm. I ran back and got a hold of the wheel quickly correcting our direction and catching the wind again.

"Aha!" I yelled. "You got that?" I added yelling to Booger who was now hoisting the main sail.

"Think so," he said grunting as he pulled the main line down hoisting the main sail up.

"You got it. Tie it down and get over here," I said.

The sail went up and we took off our fastest speed yet about 6.7 mph from just the wind pushing us.

"Grab the wheel, mate!" I said to Booger loudly over the sound of us crushing the waters.

"Okay!" he said joyfully. It may have been his first time sailing the ship and it was a great time to do it, this was the epitome of "smooth sailing."

"You good?" I asked.

"Yeah, where you going?" Booger asked nervously.

"To pack us a bowl, matey," I said smiling.

"Nice!" he replied sounding stoked and continued steering the ship without a care in the world.

A few minutes later when I came back out with a cherried bowl I could see he was clearly enjoying the moment as he dramatically steered and overacted the part of sailor steering a vessel like we were in a storm.

I smiled to myself and said, "Quickly, hit it while it's going," referring to the slowly dying cherried bowl.

"EYE," he yelled like a pirate and snatched the piece dramatically stoking it to keep it alive. He puff puff puffed and it was good again and he coughed steering and blowing smoke behind us.

"Epic shit!" I said. "Right brudda?" nudging him with my elbow and trying to get his attention but he was focused.

"Crazy," he said without looking at me. He had a job to do and he was doing it no room for distractions. He handed the pipe back.

"Keep killing it man," I said taking a seat on the high side bench next to him.

The high side is the side that's high up in the air because the boat is leaning towards the other side. It helps offset the balance sitting there and is generally drier. I sat and smoked observing as we sailed and thought how perfect it was for Booger to get this night. Night sailing isn't always easy and he had the glassy, flat water, calm breeze at our back, and a full moon. It does not get better than that. And I was happy for him.

It seemed like Booger had it under control. I finished the pipe and switched over to the low side.

"Booger dude, you gonna be alright if I close my eyes for a bit?" I asked him but I knew the answer.

"Yup," he said.

"Awesome. Wake me when you need me," I said to him as I laid down and tried to get comfy.

I know I had been sleeping more than anyone but since this was all my idea I felt responsible for everyone's lives. It was a lot more serious and more stress than I had expected. The stress and stuff maybe made me more tired, but I also felt I need to be able to watch over both day and night shifts as much as possible, so sleeping while things were copascetic meant I could be ready and awake while they were chaotic. It made sense to me and it felt good, too. I woke sporadically with splashes to the face until I couldn't take it anymore.

"Alright, I'm up," I said, half drenched. Booger looked beat and the sky was starting to lighten up as the sun ascended in the distance over the vast ocean before me.

He looked at me as if to say, "Finally," but the words that came out were, "Wanna switch?"

"Eye," I said and took my position at the helm. Booger went to take my previous position on the low-side bench. "Don't do it, mate. Just go inside, I'll handle this for a while," I said.

"Are you sure?" Booger asked.

"Yeah. You'll just get all wet there," I said reassuring him.

"Cool, let me know," and he went down into the cabin.

I figured it was a good time to cover some ground so to speak and let them all rest while sails were set and we were cruising right along. Standing at the helm, holding the wheel that controls our direction, our fate, our destiny, it felt powerful. Powered, pushed, and propelled by the wind through this liquid body that makes up so much of our world, travelling freely. There was and is nothing like it. We had been sailing for two days and two nights now straight going onto our third day of our first ever voyage.

I began wondering if we were still going the right way or if we would be there soon. Our phones no longer got service so we were very far out. We were still heading south directly so at very least I figured we'd hit Cuba if we went too far. We weren't just sailing randomly. I had planned it out, but what if I planned it wrong?

DAY 11

I started to get a little nervous and the water got choppier as the sun came up.

"Guys," I yelled. "Guys," I yelled again a little louder. "Yo dudes!" I shouted at the cabin door and I heard a muffled bunch of

"Be right there!" and "Coming!" shouted back.

The crew emerged jostled and concerned as they quickly filed out from below deck.

"What's up?" Dave asked rubbing the sleep out of his eyes.

"What do you need!?" Booger came shouting out next and Sean was there ready for whatever he was told.

"Get me the pipe and make sure it's packed," I told Booger who looked like he realized it wasn't anything crazy or at least we weren't in trouble so he was relieved but maybe annoyed, but I wasn't done yet.

"Haha," Sean laughed. "Is that it? Wake and bake!" he exclaimed joyously.

"Uh, well sit down, boyO's," I said in my pirate voice nervously about to break the bad news to them.

Sean and Dave looked at each other and sat. Booger came out and handed me the pipe.

"You spark it," I said pushing it back as I steered obviously unable to light it.

"What's up?" Booger asked curiously sensing something was indeed wrong and put the pipe and lighter down.

Dave grabbed it, "Yeah, c'mon, what's up?" he said taking a hit and passing it to Sean.

"Well, um, you see boys," I started.

"Come on, out with it," Booger snapped.

"We might be lost," I said flatly as the boat continued speeding to an unknown destination.

And it was suddenly no joke. We all felt the reality of the surreal situation.

"What!? How!?" Booger barked angrily in his floppy hat.

"I don't know, I mean we should be there by now, I think," I said.

"Well, we did spend that day floating mostly," Dave said.

"Yeah," Sean said nodding.

"True, but still," I said, not sure, "What are we like 30-50 miles off shore?" I asked.

"Last time I checked, GPS said 29 miles out, but then we floated and the batteries are dead now," Booger said.

We continued passing the pipe around and all took some nice wake and bake hits silently thinking. We knew if we called someone for help like the coast guard that would be the end of the trip and cost us money or something. It was a bummer to think it was over before it even started, before we could find Sensemilla Island or even really look.

"Let's go a few more hours and see how we feel then," I said.

"Yeah maybe we'll still get there soon," Dave said.

"Okay," Booger said begrudgingly.

"I'm gonna pack another bowl," Sean said and went below deck.

"I'm going to rest for a bit," and I followed Sean.

"You good?" he asked when I met him down there while he packed the bowl.

I said yeah, but he could tell something was wrong.

"Alright man, rest up, I'll wake you when we get there, ha," he said laughing.

"Where Cuba?" I replied.

"Sensemilla Island!" he said going back up top with the others.

I laughed and rolled over to sleep off some stress that I was leading my crew, my friends, astray, the wrong way. Suddenly, I was being violently awakened by a very excited Sean who was shaking me and jumping up and down screaming.

"A boat! A boat!"

I opened my eyes, "What kind of boat?" I asked without moving but answered quickly.

"A big one," he replied and I looked at him to see he was wide-eyed and anxious for me to do something.

"Let me see," I jumped up and hurried up top to see what it was.

We hadn't seen anyone so far, so this was new for us and gave us hope that we were at least close to somewhere maybe.

"Where is it?" I called out and climbed up to the bow where Booger was hanging on to the rails of the bowsprit trying to get a good look at the boat.

I could see it far, far in the distance riding the horizon from right to left.

"That's not a boat. That's a big ship, like a cruise ship!" I yelled to the crew. "Switch the sails, let's get closer," I yelled again and they all started moving.

Sean and Booger got the smaller skinnier front sail that was meant for speed and set it up like professionals while I took the helm from Dave and told him to roll one up for us. "And find me some binoculars," I thought I had seen some on the ship somewhere.

Once again the sails were set with the intentions of getting somewhere as we chased down this sign of life in the shape of a ship that could keep our dreams of finding the island afloat. Dave came up with a doobie burning and some old crusty binoculars around his neck that must have come with our boat.

"Here you go, bro," he said looking stoney and delirious as he wobbled from the motion of us increasing speed and handed me the stuff.

"Eye, thank you!" I shouted. "Go lay down," I yelled over the wind putting the binoculars around my neck and joint in my mouth as it burned away rapidly dissolving in the wind. I knew that was going to happen, but I wanted it so fuck it – smoke it while you got it, would suck more to have it all taken away.

"I'm good, I'll lay here," he said laying on the low side and instantly regretting it, "Never mind," and Dave went down into the cabin to sleep.

"Haha," I laughed as he closed the old wooden double doors to the cabin that reminded me somewhat of an old western saloon swinging doors.

We were heeled over and hauling ass going fast as fuck, straight for the vessel getting closer and closer.

"Someone take the helm," I yelled and Booger came running.

"Got it," he said.

"Good job, mate, I'm going to see if I can see what it is," I said, thinking I don't want to steer us straight into the Coast Guard or something.

I ran up to the front where Sean was now hanging on as we tore through the open ocean, water splashing up around us with each random wave we bashed through.

"Oy," I shouted at him, handing him the joint.

"EYE," he yelled back, we both smiled hanging on for dear life.

"Where is it now?" I asked.

"There," he pointed a little to the left of where we were heading. We needed to adjust sails again. It was really moving East fast. I held up the binoculars with one hand holding on with the other.

"Island Express," I could read it clear as the day was bright and sunny.

"Follow that ship!" I yelled and ran back to the helm adjusting the sails and took over from Booger.

"What's going on?" Booger looked concerned whether he should be happy or worried.

"That's it, BoyO!" I yelled at him.

"What's it?" Booger snapped back.

"Island Express, it says. Island Express!" I shouted.

Sean and Booger cheered. It meant we were going the right way and we were very close now.

"What is it? What is it?" Dave came out to see us cheering and wanted to know the news, but he already knew it was good as he joined in the celebration.

"Island Express!" Sean and Booger yelled as Sean passed what was left of the doobie and I steered us towards our destiny.

We were behind it now, heading straight East with the "Island Express" landing at whatever island it was going to. We were catching up cutting it off diagonally, but in the same direction we were no match for the Island Express as it took off, and we continued in that direction knowing it was up there ahead somewhere. The wind was still on our side, pushing us constantly and soon enough for the first time in three days it was there.

"LAND HO," Sean hollered from the bow causing Dave and Booger to rush up and get a look for themselves. We had made it to where exactly we weren't sure but within a few hours we knew we could be standing on it, thankful to be alive and off the boat.

"What should we do?" Booger came back and asked me.

"Prepare to go ashore," I yelled like a pirate.

"EYE!" they all yelled.

They all went down below deck, I think just to smoke and maybe eat, I'm not sure, but I sat there at the helm relieved. I had successfully done at least part of what I set out to do and no one died. The moment I was having as I sailed our ship towards this new land is almost indescribable. I felt a sudden random relation to what I imagined original explorers who found these lands and what emotions they felt.

The land became closer and closer bigger and bigger until there were no longer images of islands in the distance. There was real land in front of me and then on either side as I started sailing between two islands that were close enough to throw a rock at.

"We're here!" I yelled and they emerged in a cloud of smoke and excitement as they each ran to a side to look around.

"WHOAH," Sean yelled.

"WHAT! This is crazy," Dave said and Booger was speechless.

"We did it boys! Take down the sails," I ordered. We were barely getting wind and I had kicked on the engine 20 minutes ago just to speed things up.

Sean and Dave took down the front sail. Booger dropped and folded the main and covered it up.

On one side was an uninhabited looking island about a football field in length surrounded by anchored boats. On the other side was an island of equal size covered in billion-dollar houses and we were cruising right between them.

In front of us not much further was land so I passed the islands to get to the mainland where there was a very high wall with a cruise ship docked at it.

"Where should we go?" I yelled to the crew who was scattered on the boat and they all came back to the helm as I motored past the gigantic cruise ship.

"I see a spot up ahead," Booger said and he ran back up to the bow. "Yeah right up here, slow it down," he said.

"Go see if he's right," I said to Dave and Sean who followed Booger up to see.

"Yeah right here, slow down," Dave said confirming a spot to dock.

The wall was too high and seemed to only be for cruise ships. It was impossible to dock there so I was hoping this was right for our tiny boat.

"K," I yelled slowing the engine to almost neutral and beginning to see the entrance to this unknown inlet, but it had to be for boats, and it looked good, so I pulled in between the opening in the giant concrete wall, trying to avoid hitting the sides of our vessel on the concrete but it seemed we had plenty of room.

"Nice!" Booger cheered.

I put the engine in neutral and steered carefully toward the protruding wooden dock in this strange dead-end inlet.

"Get ready to tie her down!" I shouted and they all looked at me ready to jump the fuck off this thing. I lined her up and then put it in reverse to kill the momentum as we pulled up alongside this beautiful wooden dock, clean and pristine.

"GO!" I shouted. "GO."

They jumped off to tie us down but I had too much momentum and I hit hard into the dock making a horrible noise.

"She okay?" one of the boys said.

"What the fuck?" I think Booger said.

I went to check it out as they started to tie us down. It was just a bent bowsprit luckily and the boat and we were safe.

As I looked around, it all became real.

"Oh my dudes!" I said to the crew.

There were stores or condos all around this boardwalk like area that we just pulled up and pirated. It was clearly a very ritzy area that we probably weren't supposed to be at, but as we looked around and saw the magical sparkling tropical blue green see-through water, we all looked at each other and knew what to do. Sean, Dave, Booger and I celebrating our achievements jumped in doing front flips and cannonballs.

The celebrations were cut short when our boat began getting thrashed by large waves apparently coming from the incoming cruise ships.

"Fuck, what's happening?!" Dave yelled.

"I don't know. Let's go!" I yelled back and I hopped back in the driver's seat. "Untie us! Quickly!" almost screaming suddenly as the beating became harder.

BASH! BASH! Splash. The boat was being crashed into the dock and as the giant waves came in, they would lift us up and as they would leave, they would drop us down so low the ropes got tight.

"It's too tight!" Sean said.

"Cut the lines," I yelled, and Dave cut the lines quickly, "Get on."

The boys jumped in and we took off but as I looked back, I realized that wasn't the only bad thing we had evaded. A golf cart with two official looking people were racing towards us yelling and shaking their fists.

"Haha well, that was fun," I laughed.

"Bahaha," they all laughed seeing what I saw behind us.

"Where do we go now?" Booger asked.

"I don't know," I replied. "We gotta find a place to anchor," realizing as I said it that the sun was setting and we had never anchored before.

"Prepare the anchor!" I yelled out.

"Where's the anchor?" Booger asked.

"Up at the front, wedged tight in the bowsprit," I said amazed he hadn't seen it. It wasn't big, but it had been there all along.

"I seen it," Sean said looking ready for action.

"Good, go get it out and pull up 7-10 times the depth we are at in length of chain," I said trying to make it clear from what I picked up researching on the phone one night for a moment.

"Uh, why don't you just do it?" Booger asked.

"Because I have something important to do here while the anchor is being thrown, I need to reverse the engine once it grabs to make it lock into the ground better, so we don't move," I explained as we headed for a spot.

I wanted something close to land so we didn't have to dinghy over a long distance.

"Oh, sorry, ok, I'm going to help him," Booger said, looking ashamed for questioning me.

"All good man," I said to Booger. "Hey Dave, will you clean up the pipes and stuff in case we run into trouble?" I said.

"Yup," he said dusting off some ashes near him and picking up our recent roach before he went down into the cabin.

"Nice, thanks," I said now looking for the perfect spot, slowly trolling through what must have been a channel for cruise ships.

"How's that look?" Sean yelled and I saw he was pointing to a small fleet of about eight sailboats anchored and moored at a strategically close looking area, not far from a marina. We didn't want the marina obviously. That would cost money we didn't really have but anchoring across from it with these boats was free.

"Let's do it, looks good," I said getting ready for this new part of the journey I hadn't been looking forward to for some reason and changing course in the direction of what might be our new home for a while.

I slowed down as we approached, but it felt like there was no room for us. I continued maneuvering around the other vessels until I came to what seemed like a big enough clearing. We needed to leave enough space for our boat to float around in any direction from the anchor and not hit anyone else's boat. I put it in neutral and started floating towards the center of the open area.

"You ready?" I yelled

"Where do I throw it?" Sean yelled back almost frantically.

"Straight ahead," I shouted realizing I hadn't relayed enough of what was going on.

"NOW!" I yelled but it was too late. We were too close to the next vessel.

"K," he said.

"Nope, too late," I hollered and redirected the ship turning it around and lined it up again slowly.

"Alright, toss it in the center of this area and then hold on while I reverse to lock it in," I said trying to be more clear.

"K, I'll try," Sean said.

I figured I'd let that one slide, there was no time to correct that we don't "try" we only "do."

"K, now," I shouted and he tossed the anchor into the water. I waited for it to settle and the chain to slow down and then I gassed it in reverse, whipping the boat fast backwards until it felt like the boat literally and physically hit a wall and came to a halt just full speed going nowhere.

"Yes!" I shouted.

"Yaay," cheers came from the boat, but it was too dark now to even see who was saying what.

"Good job."

"We did it."

"Let's smoke."

"Let's party."

A range of commentary and emotions came from the crew as we had just successfully completed our first leg of this wild journey we had embarked on, when everything else told us we couldn't do it or we were crazy, well we were there and it gave me and all of us I'm sure a new confidence we had never felt, anchored at our new home in the islands.

"Roll one up?" Dave said flipping the lights on.

"Yehhess," I said feeling like I could finally relax for the first time in who knows how long now.

"We did it," Booger said. It must have been him earlier too, he was so glad we just didn't die out there.

"Yes we did, Booger my dude," I said chugging some sweet corn juice water from the can left over earlier. "You guys killed it, we killed it. I'm proud of us," I said.

"Spark it up, Captain," Dave said and handed me the fresh blunt he just rolled.

"EYE," I said with a sigh as I sat back, stretched, and lit it. "Thank ya matey," I said smiling exhausted.

"Thank you, mate," Dave said and we all smoked sitting on the benches around the helm, silhouettes of ourselves backlit by the gold antique glow of our ship's cabin lights.

"Is that boat getting closer?" I said laughing. I was relaxed but hadn't fully let my guard down. It was hard to believe that I even could.

"Nah, you're just seeing things," Dave said laughing.

I tried to measure by holding my thumb up and seeing if it was moving but the current had all the boats moving, a little left and right. It was too hard to tell and I was delirious.

"Okay, bedtime," I said out loud but it was really meant to be an internal thought.

"Aw really?" Sean said. "You're probably right though," he said sounding sad the party was over.

"Yeah man, I'm beat but you guys can stay up. Do whatever," I said starting to head into the cabin. "Plus, we got a lot of exploring to do tomorrow. We might even go on a walkabout," I added.

"Yeah, true," Dave said.

"Word," Sean said and we hadn't realized but Booger had already fallen asleep right there on the bench.

"Night dudes," I said.

"Night brudda," Sean and Dave said.

"We did it!" Booger mumbled in his sleep and we killed the lights and passed out.

Maybe an hour or so later I woke up with a bad feeling. I went out onto the deck to check if we had moved and Booger who was still outside sleeping on the bench woke up.

"What are you doing?" he whispered without budging and it sounded painful.

"Checking to see if we moved," I whispered back. It was so hard to tell because all the boats moved with the current together.

"Did we?" he replied sounding more concerned.

"I can't tell," I said back quickly but trying not to sound worried.

"It's fine, man, we did it," Booger answered calmly falling back asleep.

What was I worrying about? Booger didn't even care. I felt like I must be going crazy. I must just need rest and went back to sleep on my bench in the cabin, but I couldn't sleep. I felt restless and worried and by the grace of God I decided to check again even though I was exhausted I got up and went out to see. We were mere inches from colliding and possibly damaging some sailor stranger's boat likely a vagabond pirate such as ourselves.

I didn't even wake the boys. I just turned on the engine and started moving and they woke up and ran out.

"What's going on!?" Booger sat up disturbed from his slumber.

"We were about to hit that boat," I said. "Pull up the anchor when I get above it and we'll try again," I yelled and the crew snapped to it.

Sean and Dave hoisted the anchor up and I redirected the ship, lining it up all over again. It honestly felt like a nightmare.

Alright, throw it in there good!" I shouted with no regard for our possibly sleeping neighbors.

"Throwing," Sean yelled.

Again I felt it settle and gassed it hard in reverse to get a tight grip. I'd never done it before but it felt right. We were in reverse and not moving because the anchor was working, or so we thought because as I continued to wake up through the night I could see we were moving again. I let them sleep until we got too close and had to move again, clearly this was not the spot. I started the engine again and they all woke up.

"Again, really?" Dave said.

"Fuck this spot," Booger said.

"Someone just grab the fucking anchor so we can get a few more hours of sleep and the sun will be up," I expressed what seemed to be a new plan.

"K," Sean said and we did it all again and again. It felt fine but I knew it wasn't.

I didn't even go to sleep and just smoked on the deck alone because Booger had gone into the cabin. I was pissed. I was bummed. I went from such a high to such a low so fast, but I did need to put that aside and make a plan.

Day 12

The sun started to rise and the colors of reds, orange, pink, and yellow painted a beautifully trippy background behind the island we had passed when we first came in, surrounded by boats. It was further away but that must be the reason there were so many boats there. As the sun rose over the island and our boat neared the next boat, I knew that little island in the sun was the answer.

"Wake up men!" I yelled. "Time to move to our new home," I shouted trying to wake them and get this show on the road. "Come on guys, let's go!" I said firing up the engine.

Booger came running out, "Aw man, we're so close to shore though," he cried out, clearly wanting to just walk around on solid ground. We all did.

"I know, Boog, but we gotta get settled somewhere. If we go to land with our boat like this it will float away or hit someone and then we owe them, got it?" I said getting frustrated and idling forward towards the anchor. "Can you pull up the anchor?" I asked Booger.

He didn't want to admit he couldn't so he stuttered for a moment. "I, I… I can," he sputtered.

"Ok, good, go ahead," I ordered knowing one of the others would come up to help.

"Coming," Sean shouted and he stumbled out of the cabin and onto the deck scurrying to help Booger.

"Hah, nice, thank you," I said to Sean who ran to the bow and started pulling all the old rusty chain up and then the anchor. Booger got out of the way. It wasn't easy and every time he got covered in rust stains.

"FREE is free," Sean yelled back.

"Hang on," I shouted up at them and started motoring out of this horrible little spot where the anchor never anchored and I never slept.

The sun was still coming up and it was a beautiful day ahead. The waters began catching light and illuminated a brilliant aqua marine under us, clear as the clearest best HD image with infinite pixels. We could see we were passing over massive reefs with tons of life all around. We had only seen this on TV or in aquariums but this wasn't man made.

"Dave!" I yelled.

"He's out," Sean laughed.

"Dude, you gotta see this," I yelled again and Dave finally woke and came out.

"What man?" he said.

"Look at that shit," I said pointing over the edge.

He lit up with amazement and ran to the side. "Holy fuck!" he shouted. "That's some National Geographic shit," he said.

"Haha yep," I said and we all laughed, looking around and taking in the scenery of where we were.

I was going very slow so not to disturb the reef life as we approached the little island surrounded by boats. I went between them and the island which was very shallow, but our boat had a two foot draft. I had heard before we left that this boat would be a good "island hopper" because it can go shallow with a draft like that.

We all looked nervous as we cruised the shallow waters, but when we came around the corner to the sunny side of the island, there it was, a spot with our names on it, a random gap in the boats at the front meant for us.

"You think it's good?" Booger asked because it was almost too good to be true.

"Whaddaya mean?" I asked.

"Like what if it's another ship's spot?" he said back.

"Hmmm. We'll just have to see," I said smiling. "Prepare the anchor!" I yelled unnecessarily, but I was happy, this could be it, the spot for a while. I needed a break. We all did.

Sean and Dave ran to the front.

"Get ready," I yelled then flipped the engine to neutral, crawling towards our new anchorage. "Toss it, now!" I hollered and they did. I let it settle a moment and then gassed it full throttle reverse.

CHUNK!

The boat lurched and we all wobbled almost falling. Booger might have fallen.

"WOW!" Booger said angrily.

"I think it worked," I said laughing and Sean and Dave came back laughing to the helm.

"Now what?" Booger asked sounding bored or something.

"Now I relax and take care of myself. You should do the same," I said matter of factly to Booger and the boys.

"We're not going to land?" Booger said sounding frustrated now, while Sean and Dave went down into the cabin probably to smoke and eat, what I would be doing in a minute if Booger would shut up.

"To go to land we need to dinghy first of all, to dinghy I have to transfer this engine onto the dinghy unless we want to paddle, and it will take an hour. And finally, it costs money which we are very low on and need for gas. So no, Booger, we aren't going to land right away, man. Just relax, rest, smoke, drink, eat, and be merry as they say, fore we are in Paradise!" I finished by pointing at the sun and the island and the water and then just waved my arms around in extra frustration.

"Fine," he said and sat down on the deck bench crossing his arms.

I think he may have been becoming a bit delirious, maybe what I've heard referred to as "cabin fever" but we were all experiencing the same thing and I needed to focus on me for what felt like the first time in a long time.

I left him there and went down into the cabin where I found Sean and Dave smoking, eating, and drinking.

"Ahhhhh," I let out a long breathy sigh and dropped onto a bench seat. My body was tired from head to toe to fingertips and my mind was equally beat.

"This is fucking crazy!" Dave said.

"Haha yeah," Sean laughed shoving crackers in his face. "I didn't think we were really going to end up at an island," he continued munching and laughing.

I could hear them talking as I started to doze off.

"Na wake up man, we're here," Dave said nudging my lifeless body.

"What are we doing?" I said barely able to hold my eyes open.

"We wanna check out the island," Dave said.

"Yeah let's go, it's right there!" Sean exclaimed.

"Who's paddling?" I responded blankly.

"I will," Sean said sounding excited.

"Alright," I said, "Roll a doobie to smoke on the island. I'll prepare the dinghy," I added starting to like the sounds of this excursion. I just had to get the paddles really and make sure it was all good.

"Ready boys!" I yelled as I hopped into the dinghy and held onto our boat waiting for them to get in.

I already knew Booger wasn't coming even though he wanted to go to land so bad. He meant civilization not just solid ground like we all needed, but I asked anyway.

"You coming, Boog. Doobie on the island?" I asked shortly.

"Na, I'm good," he said.

"Cool, we need someone to watch the boat really," I said and Dave and Sean came out.

"Let's do this," Dave said pushing behind Sean as they fought to get in the dinghy.

"Calm down boys, we'll be there soon," I said laughing.

"Not soon enough," Sean said and they both climbed down into the dinghy laughing.

"Got the stuff?" I asked.

"Yup," Sean said.

"And we're off," I said pushing off from the boat instantly feeling a freeing feeling not having to be the one responsible for the boat.

Dave and Sean each picked up an oar and began rowing us to shore. It was probably 200 feet away. I sat back letting them take control. I couldn't get over how crazy the water was, how freaking clear it was and the sea life, the fish, and the sting rays and reefs and shells of every color, blues of every hue and vibrant yellow schools of fish passed under us like it was a game to them. We were now inches above the white sand in water so clear we appeared to be hovering above our shadow.

"What do we do?" Sean asked.

"Hop out," I said laughing. We were all out of it, mentally tired from the trip, we all laughed as we stepped out of the life boat and into the warm tropical water and dragged the boat up on to shore.

"Haha!"

"Aha!" The three of us jumped around and laughed rejoicing and stomping on the sand. It was like when we hit the first dock but we felt like no one could stop us now.

"Dudes!" I yelled.

"Duude!" they yelled back and we noticed Booger on the ship waving and we all waved back.

"This is crazy," Dave said. "Thank you man," he added looking at me.

"No thank you dudes, couldn't have done it without you," I said smiling and Sean pulled out the doobie and lit it.

We sat down and smoked looking out at the sea we sailed lit by the vastly infinite blue sky and in the foreground our little sailboat that carried us all the way.

When the joint was gone we were still chilling, not moving, just soaking up the sun on solid ground, sprawled out on the thin beach that I assumed went all around the little island. It was a perfect little beach with shells and coral pieces all around and driftwood logs. I took one of the pieces of coral and put it in my dreads, it was like a perfect bead.

"We could sell these," I said laughing and making sure it was in there good. I was kind of joking but at the same time started really thinking what we could do for money around here.

"You think?" Dave asked.

"I don't know haha," I laughed again.

Sean got up and started walking into the island it looked like.

"Where you goin'?" I shouted.

"Piss," he yelled back and went into the bush.

I turned to Dave, "Should we go exploring or wait for Booger?" I asked what he thought.

"Someone's gotta stay on the boat," he said lifting his head and then putting it back down enjoying the moment too much to care, but he was right.

"That's true though," I said.

"Hey, check this out!" Sean yelled.

"What is it?" I yelled back not really wanting to move yet.

"A whole kayak," he said back.

"What really?" I said and hopped up to check it out.

"Yeah, looks good, too," he said.

It was a nice looking but used red sea kayak either washed up or strategically placed, but either way I got a weird feeling.

"Hmmm that's weird …" I said. "Cool, but weird," I repeated.

"Why?" Sean said.

"Oh wow, cool," Dave said coming over and joining us.

"Yeah but let's just leave it alone in case someone's here somewhere," I said and we all looked at each other eerily.

"Hello!" Sean called out

"No man, shh, I don't want them to know we're here if they are," I said whispering.

"Haha what's the problem?" Dave said.

"Pirates," I said in my pirate voice and they understood. "Let's go on a little walkabout and see if we find anybody," I said quietly now and they looked excited but maybe nervous as well.

There was basically an impression of a path leading from the kayak in the bush deeper into the island. I started pushing my way through the palms and the spikey bushes where the trails became more defined suddenly.

"Oh there's definitely people out here," I said, starting to walk more cautiously.

"GaAAH," Sean let out a roar and fell to his ass clutching his foot in pain.

"What happened?" I asked.

"You good," Dave added quickly.

"Fuck dude, I stepped on something sharp," groaning and holding up his foot to show us, "Is it bad?" he asked.

Me and Dave cringed at the sight of his grotesquely lacerated heel.

"Ooooh, um, yeah, let's wrap that up," I said handing him my bandana.

"Ah," he let out another painful sigh as he wrapped it tight.

"It'll be alright. It's not that bad," I said handing him a big stick. "Here use this as a crutch," I said trying to accommodate him so we could keep searching.

"Thanks," he said sounding down.

"You wanna go on or go back?" I asked him not really caring what Dave thought.

"I'm good, let's check it out," Sean said trying to perk up.

"Alright nice," I said, leading us further into unknown territories.

We were walking down long skinny winding trails that seemed to lead nowhere. I put my arms out and stopped us all dead in our tracks. Up ahead I could see a couple of human-like shapes moving about.

"Ahoy!" I didn't hesitate and yelled at them. They froze.

"Ahoy!" they yelled back and started toward us.

"Why'd you do that?" Dave elbowed me in the side whispering.

"We need to assert ourselves, act tough," I said under my breath as they got closer and we all puffed up our chests.

I had made the split-second decision by running different scenarios through my mind and that one played out the best.

"Pirates are like animals, the way they can sense fear," I said one last thing before they were right in front of us.

"Thought you were the cops," the tall one said.

"Haha yeah, we don't like them around here," the short one said almost threateningly like we might be under cover.

"Haha na just sailors searching for square grouper," I said and Sean and Dave started laughing awkwardly trying to follow my lead.

I wanted to test them and see if they knew anything about weed washing up or maybe they would have clues to Sensemilla Island. If they knew what a square grouper was, they were cool with me, otherwise maybe they were the undercovers.

"Haha oh yeah we were just about to smoke a bowl," the tall one said. "Name's Slice," he added stretching out a dirty, rough hand to shake and I reached mine out to see they were comparably equal in crustiness.

"Joe," I said. "And this is Dave and Sean," I said pointing each out. They smiled and nodded, me and Slice still held hands.

"This is my kid brother, Dukey," Slice pointed with his head.

"Hi, nice to me ya. Wanna see the club house?" the short, chunkier one asked and Slice finally let go.

"Ya, for sure!" I replied acting excited, but inside I was very worried.

These dudes were much older than us and we had no clue why they were here. They knew we were looking for weed, but what if they were looking for more people to kill? A couple of murderers on the run. I did have a large knife on my hip and there were three of us and only two of them. I caught a look from Dave as we followed them to the their "club house" in the middle of this random little island off the coast we thought was uninhibited.

"How far," I asked after only a few steps.

"Oh it's right up here," Slice said over his shoulder still leading us through the island.

The shrubbery and foliage started to thin out and I could see a tarp strung up in some trees above a little clearing ahead. As we got closer, I could see there were tables, chairs, a guitar, and a little fire pit. They really had a club house fort area out here in the middle of nowhere.

"Here we are," Slice said. "Welcome in. Take a seat.

I didn't really want to sit but I was so tired I had to.

"You guys say something about smoking?" Slice said and got all of our attention as he lit a pipe and smoked it.

"Yeah!" we all said

"Here ya go," Slice passed me the pipe.

"Thank you," I said, taking a hit. "Mmm," I added and passed it to Sean who was sitting in a rickety old lawn chair next to me.

"So this washed up or is it from the mainland?" I asked straight up. I wasn't pussy-footing anymore. It was straight to business for me.

"This did wash up 'bout a month ago and it's almost gone," Slice said.

My heart sunk. I was suddenly having trouble breathing. Was this it? Already claimed by these two marauders? I felt my heart rate increase and grow louder pounding in my ear. I looked at Sean and Dave who looked like I felt.

"That's crazy," I finally mustered up the strength to say words.

"You need a drink?" Dukey asked lifting a tapestry that was draped over some crates to reveal brand new bottles of soda, every type and munchies, all the best kinds, name-brand, expensive stuff.

"Uh, I'm good. We're good, actually we better get back to our friend on the boat," I said, but really I wanted it all and I could tell Sean and Dave did too, but they followed my lead and we started leaving.

"Thanks for everything. It was nice meeting you guys," I said.

"Yup, nice meeting you," Dave said and Sean waved.

"Yeah, great meeting you. Come back some time, we do movie nights on Fridays," Dukey and Slice waved back and we headed down the windy paths trying to find our way back to our dinghy.

I started moving faster hoping to jog my memory, but nothing looked familiar.

"This doesn't look right," I could hear Dave yelling up to me as we jogged and jumped through the branches.

"Whoah, my bad," Sean said, bumping into me as I suddenly stopped and put my hand up to silence them but it was too late.

"HELLO," an old voice cackled from a popup tent in front of us. "Who is it?" the voice called out again more agitated from our lack of response.

"Haha, hello," I said. "We are new here. Just checking out the island."

A very, very old withered sun-dried looking lady climbed out wearing I'm not sure, a strange mixture of clothes she found that had washed up maybe, I don't know.

"Oh, hi, I'm Shelly," she said looking perhaps happy to see new faces.

We introduced ourselves and talked for a quick minute and she let us know we were welcome to set up our site near her if we'd like because someone recently left and there was an opening. We said thanks and told her we'd tell our friend on the boat and see what he thinks, but we were already sure we weren't doing that as we continued around the outside of the island.

"Definitely not staying on this island," Dave said.

"Nope, definitely not," I said.

"This place is a trip," Sean said. He had been very quiet. I think we were all just taking it in.

"Look," I pointed at what looked like a shop of some sort, almost like a tropical tiki bar but as it came into sight there were tools and engines and gasoline cans laying around. It was more like a mechanic shop right here on the island. We ran over and started checking it out.

"Maybe we can get stuff fixed here if we need to," Dave said.

"Yeah, maybe," I said but I had that bad feeling again. "Let's keep moving," I added.

"Yeah I'm hungry," Sean said and we continued around the island eventually making it back over to where we started and I could see the dinghy still sitting there on the beach in the hot sun.

"Man the island feels bigger than it looks," Dave said.

"Yeah but that was good to get a feel for it," I said remembering that those dudes said that weed washed up here.

"Yeah," Sean said sounding low on energy and maybe in pain from the foot thing.

"Hey, you guys think this is Sensemilla Island?" I asked.

"I was thinking the same thing," Dave said.

"Those dudes had everything right there in their club house," I said.

"I imagined it to have more than just one random pound," Sean said.

"Yeah but even one random pound washing up every once in a while is pretty crazy," I said.

"How'd they get all that stuff out there?" Dave asked.

"I don't know man. I don't know," I said feeling confused about the whole thing. "Aw fuck," I said approaching the dinghy.

"What?" Dave asked.

"What?" Sean repeated because I hadn't answered fast enough.

"Look, it's losing air," I said, kicking at the dinghy.

"Fuck!" Dave exclaimed and I sighed.

"We had a dinghy patch kit somewhere on the boat, but someone needed to go get it and some soap to find the hole.

"Who's going?" I asked and we looked around.

"Can't Booger bring it over?" Dave asked.

"I'll just go get it," Sean said, "I'm hungry anyway."

"Cool," I said. "We'll be here waiting," I added and he ran into the water and swam off to our boat.

I jumped into the water, too and washed off a little. Dave ran and jumped in, "Cannon ball!" he screamed disturbing the tropical oasis. We both laughed. We swam for a little bit then got out and dried off under the remaining hours of sunlight hoping Sean would be back soon.

"Got it," I opened my eyes to see Sean dripping over me holding the stuff we needed.

"Good man," I said joyfully and bounced up to start the job. Dave got up and dapped Sean.

"Word, did you bring more weed?" he asked.

"Hah, you know it," Sean said.

"Niiice, haha," Dave and I said.

"Fire it up, I'll get this started, hopefully we have enough daylight," I said, starting to cover the dinghy with soap.

Then I dragged it into the water and instantly started bubbling from the right side but was coming from underneath. I flipped it over and there was a mass of bubbles coming from one spot.

"Found it," I said. "Help me lift it out and onto shore. Maybe we put a hole in it dragging it up earlier."

"K," Sean and Dave said, Sean handed me the doobie and they both lifted it out and placed it on shore gently.

"Nice, thank you," I said handing the doobie back that was basically a roach already and Sean hit it again then put it out next to him on a log. I had just put the gluey patch onto the puncture spot of our lifeboat when…

"Freeze!" a voice demanded and that sinking feeling hit again, twice in one day, maybe I shouldn't have ignored the signs. I looked up to see a squad of swat-like authorities marching towards us.

"You are trespassing," the one in charge told us.

"I'm so sorry, we are just trying to fix our dinghy and get back to our boat," I said honestly and it was good enough for him I guess.

"Ok, you haven't seen anyone out here stealing engines have you?" the man asked and Sean slid the roach into the sand with his foot trying to cover it before they saw.

"No sir, we just came over to work on the dinghy on hard ground and have more space," I tried to assure the officer we had nothing to do with anything going on here.

"Ok, well don't stay here long. There's been reports of a man with a gun, mad about his engine stolen and he believes its here," the man said and handed me his card, he was the police. "Let us know if you hear anything," he added and they turned and left us.

Once they were out of sight I lost it.

"Holy Fuck Boys!" I said, "Let's get the fuck outta here."

They looked at me and we didn't even wait for the patch to dry and threw the dinghy in and paddled home to our vessel.

"Booger Dude!" I called out as we pulled up to the boat and tied on. "Booger! You missed it man." I hopped out of the dinghy and onto the deck.

"I think I'd rather have stayed here," Dave said.

"Cha same," Sean said.

I turned to help them up onto the deck but I was shocked.

"C'mon men, that was fun!" I said laughing.

"Yeah but it was fucking scary," Dave said.

"Scary?" Booger said, popping out of the cabin doors. "What the hell happened over there?"

"Bro so much," Sean said. "I didn't even start to tell you earlier so I could get back to them quick.

"Take a seat, Booger. Dave will you roll a blunt?" I said. Booger sat down on the deck bench.

"I gotta eat something," Dave said.

"I'll roll it," Sean said sounding happy for a blunt and headed into the cabin.

"Word, you making rice and beans?" I asked Dave.

"Yup," he replied and went down to start cooking.

"Nice," I said and turned to Booger, "Dude there's a tribe of homeless people living out there and they have weed and munchies and soda!" I started.

"Are you being serious?" Booger looked at me like I was joking.

"I shit you not, mate. And some old lady asked us if we wanted to set up camp by her. And then we found like a chop shop of boat engines. And then while we were smoking and fixing the dinghy, cops came and they looked like SWAT and we all talked to them but it was all good," I finished, and he looked like he was still processing everything.

"Why'd the cops come?" was the first thing he managed to say.

"I guess someone got robbed of an engine and came here looking for it with a gun," I said nonchalantly but it wasn't cool with Booger.

"What!?" Booger said standing up and looking around.

"Yeah, it's all good though man," I tried reassuring him but it was too late. I think his mind was wandering with possibilities.

"What if they come over here? Try to steal our engine?" he replied.

"We'll be here," I said.

"What about when we're not here?" he said.

"Well, when we're not here the engine will be with us on the dinghy," I said.

"What if they try and break in and steal stuff off the boat?" Booger asked. I hadn't thought of it but I sure was now.

"We'll lock it up tight, but honestly, look at us. We look like we have nothing and we were there asking for weed. They would never think we had a bunch of our own," I was now trying to convince myself as well as Booger.

"It's all good. I promise," I said but I could see he wasn't feeling it.

"K," he said and went down into the cabin.

"Good timing," Sean said, "Blunt's ready to rip," he added brandishing his fine work.

"Good, I need it," I said. "How's that rice coming?" I asked Dave.

"It'll be done by the time we smoke that," Dave replied.

"That's what's up," I said.

"Smoke on the deck?" Sean asked.

"Sure," and we all followed him up to see the most colorful sunset happening like the finale of a fireworks show, the big bang at the end of our wild day.

"Look at our backyard," and they all stared at the magically trippy vibrant fiery tones warping to one point on the horizon.

"Cheers," Sean said sparking the blunt.

"Cheers," we all said. We watched the sun go down silently smoking, each of us deep in thought. I know I was replaying everything we did to get here in my mind like a movie on fast forward.

"Dudes I'm beat," Booger said, breaking the stoney silence.

"Yeah, same," Dave said.

"I can't even lift my arms," Sean said.

"Well, let's get some sleep and come up with a plan for tomorrow," I stated.

"Sounds good," Booger said, "Night."

"Night," we all said and went to sleep.

Day 13

I don't even remember closing my eyes but the sun was up and the crew was moving about and making breakfast.

"Look who's finally up," Dave said smiling.

"Damn, I slept like a stoned baby," I replied, Sean and Dave laughed.

"How's that foot, mate?" I asked Sean.

"It's fine, salt water helped it heal fast," he said.

"Nice. What's the plan?" I asked the crew.

"Go to land," Booger called out.

"Hmm," I thought out loud. "Would be nice," I said.

"Let's do it!" Sean blurted.

"Alright, let me just get a feel for this switching engines thing," I said.

"Shit, forgot about that," Dave said. "How can we help?" he asked.

"I'm not sure yet," I answered heading out onto the deck and taking a look at the engine. "It comes off pretty easy, the hard part will be not dropping it in the ocean as I transfer it to the dinghy," I stated, climbing off the boat and into the dinghy to get a better look from down there.

"Welp, it's not happening today, boys," I said flatly as I tried to balance standing in the dinghy. "This thing's soft as a grape," I said, pressing on the side pumping it with one foot.

"Fuck that," Booger said. "I'm going to land today," he added seriously and visibly upset.

"Damn, dude, chill," Dave said looking at him with one eyebrow cocked.

"I'm sick of this shit. I wanna go," Booger said.

"We will, man, we gotta fix the dinghy first," I said. "We all wanna go to land," I added.

"Thought you fixed it yesterday," Booger complained.

"We tried to before we were so rudely interrupted by a SWAT team," I said.

There was silence for a moment and I climbed out of the dinghy and hauled it up on deck.

"We'll fix it today. We'll go tomorrow," I said. "Cool?" I asked Booger if he approved.

"Cool, yeah, whatever," he said quietly and went into the cabin.

Sean, Dave, and I looked at each other making blank clueless faces as to what Booger's problem was.

"So, we're gonna fix this thing?" Dave asked while still trying to signal me and Sean, he silently mouthed, "What was that?" so Booger didn't hear.

I put my hands up and shrugged.

"Yeah, gotta clean the wound and rebandage her," I said like a pirate loudly trying to distract from our other conversation that was happening.

Sean looked confused. "So it will be done by tonight or tomorrow?" he asked.

Me and Dave looked at each other.

"Tomorrow, if we do it right," I said.

"Oh, well what should we do today?" Sean asked.

"Just relax, enjoy it man. This is Paradise," I said gesturing to the world around us.

It was crazy the view we had of the ocean and the island across from us with the billion-dollar homes. It was like a painting and they had us for a view. It was funny to me how much they paid and the view they had of us, and how much we paid and the view we had of them.

"Word, I'm gonna smoke," Dave said.

"Same," Sean said.

"I'm gonna swim! And explore what's under our house," I said.

"Oh, shit, I might join ya," Dave said.

"Yeah," Sean yelled with excitement.

I was already wearing my swimsuit. I went and grabbed the cheap pair of snorkel goggles someone had packed and said, "See ya," as I flipped off the side of the boat. It was perfect temp bathwater and crystal clear. I opened my eyes to see the swarm of bubbles rising to the surface around me and the schools of tropical fish that I had just scared, swimming away. There was something big under me on the sea floor that looked like a reef but I could tell it wasn't.

I swam down closer, holding my breath. It was something covered in seaweed with large vines protruding and swaying in the sea current like it was alive. I was suddenly kind of freaked out but I had my boys up top. I knew I'd be alright. I went right down to it and realized it was an anchor, much larger than me.

I quickly went up for air, "Dudes!" I said bursting out of the water.

"What!?" Sean and Dave ran over to the edge.

"I found a massive anchor we can hook up to so we won't be drifting," I said splashing.

"Nice!" they yelled.

"Throw me that carabiner by the sink. I'm just going to connect our anchor chain to that one," I said remembering we had the perfect thing for this.

"Perfect," Dave said.

"Here," Sean said popping back out with the carabiner and tossing it to me.

"Wish me luck," I said and dove back down.

The anchor was alive with seaweed and sea life as I swam back down to it. It was waving its wild arms of rope overgrown by kelp as I reached out to grab some of its old chain, a lobster popped out and shocked me.

"Whoah," I said under water, losing some air and swimming backwards, but it was all good. I swam back in and continued the mission.

With our boat's anchor chain in hand still, I quickly grabbed the old chain from the found anchor and connected them. Click the carabiner snapped closed. I dropped the chains and jumped up towards the surface but the kelpy arms of the old anchor beast had grabbed hold of me, wrapping around my leg. I was feet from the surface, but I couldn't get away. I was running out of breath and started to panic. I could see Sean looking down at me waving and smiling as my life flashed before my eyes. I needed air. I suddenly realized I would die if I did not calm down and figure this out. I stopped moving and let myself sink with the water around me and calmly slid the knots off my legs of seaweed and rope that once bound me, and shot up to the surface gasping for air.

"I'm free!" I said, taking in huge amounts of oxygen and just floated on my back, staring at the sky.

"What happened? You good?" Sean said, laughing.

"Yeah, I'm good," I said laughing back, still looking at the sky, floating. "Almost just died, but I'm good," I said.

"What? What happened!?" Dave jolted back out onto the deck.

"I got wrapped up down there, almost didn't make it out," I said as I looked at him smiling a little.

"What the fuck how?" Dave asked.

"I don't know but it's all good," I said and swam back to the boat and climbed aboard, in that moment realizing I could never let my guard down while on this journey.

"Well, glad you're good dude. Sorry I didn't notice," Dave said.

"Yeah, my bad, man, I thought you were joking," Sean said.

"You saw him?" Dave asked yelling a little.

"Yeah I was waving," Sean laughed.

"Haha," I laughed shaking my head. "You almost waved goodbye," I laughed.

"Fuck dude, let's smoke," Dave said, slapping me on the back and we all laughed and smoked some weed while Booger had some alone time in the cabin.

That was enough excitement for me for the day. We spent the rest of it repairing the dinghy, smoking, eating and relaxing in Paradise our new home.

Day 14

That night I slept so good I dreamt I was home but I was awakened by the stark reality that I was still in pirate territory. A rustling noise and a clank came from the deck. Was someone trying to steal our engine. I exploded out of the cabin door, not thinking twice, and hoping to catch the thief in the act but it was only Booger who seemed to be fiddling with the engine.

"What are you doing?" I barked as he whipped around startled by my entrance.

"Just trying to understand how it works," he said back.

"Don't fuck with it, bro," I said calming down a little, knowing it wasn't an engine pirate.

"I'm not," he said. "Just wanted a better idea of how I could help get us to shore," he said.

"It's all good, man, I got it, and look at that, the dinghy is fixed," I said shocked by the sight of the fully inflated lifeboat on top of the cabin.

"How can you tell?" Booger asked, looking more happy now.

"Look it's pumped up!" I said getting louder.

I was amazed. We put the patch on but how did it inflate? I hadn't even thought of how we were going to get more air in it. We didn't have a pump.

"Nice!" Booger exclaimed. "How did it pump up?" he asked.

"I'm not sure," I said, running my hand over the hot rubber sides.

"Damn, it's hot! Maybe the sun heating it up expanded the air," I said loudly with excitement.

"Wow!" Booger said in amazement as well.

Dave and Sean must have been awakened by our commotion and excitement.

"It's good?" Dave asked springing out onto the deck.

"Yup," I said smiling from on top of the cabin now sitting with the dinghy.

"Yeww!" Sean yelled emerging from the cabin with a smoking pipe. "WakeN'Bake!" he shouted, and I threw the dinghy back in the water.

"Cheee," I said and jumped down to the deck, exchanged high fives and passed the pipe around until I was ready to give it a try.

"Alright here goes nothing," I said and I got down into the dinghy.

The crew all looked at me silently, holding their breaths as I pulled myself up to the back of our boat and held on to the engine. I stood up shakily wobbling in the dinghy, preparing to dismount our vessel's life source, an expensive piece of machinery that I couldn't drop, or we'd be screwed.

"Alright," I said again nervously. "Someone hold the dinghy steady," I shouted and Sean reached down and grabbed it, using all his strength to keep me steady while I did this.

"K, Dave get me some bungy cords and let's secure the engine to the boat in case I drop it," I ordered, and Dave grabbed some bungy cords we had and strapped it up.

"What should I do?" Booger asked.

"Put a smile on and prepare to go to land," I said and began undoing the clamps that held our engine on our boat. With a few twists it was free.

"Oh man, that was way too easy," I said.

"I wonder if they make locks for those things?" Dave said.

"We should check into that," I said. "Ready?" I asked, "One, two, threeee," I said heaving the heavier-than-expected boat engine up and off the engine mount and brought it slowly down to the back of our dinghy which had a piece of wood made for an engine to be mounted on.

"Woooo!" I shouted and breathed as I placed the motor squarely on the dinghy.

"Bang," Sean said.

"Got it, dude!" Dave yelled and Booger smiled.

"Hop in Sean, let's try her out," I said and Sean climbed in.

A couple of cranks and she started right up, "Hang on," I yelled and throttled it.

"Haha!" Sean yelled as we took off in our little lifeboat. I started weaving her through the surrounding boats and did a donut then brought her back.

"Yooo! Hah," I laughed.

"Yes!" Sean said and Dave and Booger had their arms up like we just won something. I killed the engine and tied her back up.

"Let's smoke and prepare for a proper walkabout, boys," I said in my pirate voice and asked, "Eye?"

They all yelled back in unison, "EYE!" then we broke up and started getting ready for our first-time on the new land.

"Last paper," Dave said rolling up a hefty joint.

"Alright, add it to the list. We need gas, too," I said, pulling out a gas can from under one of the deck benches. The lazarette was great storage for all our utility type stuff, ropes, tools, life jackets.

"How much money do we even have?" Dave asked.

"I have zero dollars," I said confidently.

"We got enough for gas and papers but that's about it," Booger said.

"And a burger?" Sean asked.

"Maybe," Booger said.

"Oh wow, a burger," I said, and we all started drooling.

"I stopped thinking about real food a long time ago, convinced I'd never get it again," Dave said.

"I never stopped," Sean said. "Me dreaming of burgers might be what got us here," he said laughing and we all joined in.

Dave sparked the doobie and we burned on the deck, ready to go to the mainland for the first time in what seemed like a year. I smiled looking at my motley crew of young pirates officially sailors, hair wild and gnarled, everything we owned crusty with salt and sweat.

"You dreadin' up there, mate?" I asked Booger laughing and pushed him on the shoulder.

"Yeah, kinda I guess, one started in the back," he said grabbing a massive nest at the back of his head.

"Oh ho nice!" I said and we all laughed. "Let's go," I said and hopped into the dinghy, holding it steady for the guys to get in.

"We bringing this?" Dave asked still hitting the joint.

"Hell yeah! Pass me that thing," I said and they all got in.

"You sure?" Booger asked.

"Should be good around here," I said. "Did you lock the cabin up?" I asked looking at Booger.

"Yeah, good to go," he said.

"Alright, we shall see if anyone tries anything, I got those EXPLODING TRAPS set up!" I said winking and lying in case anyone else was listening.

"Niiiice," Sean said and I handed him the doobie smirking and started the engine, she puttered a little then fired up.

"Shit, we might be low on gas," I said a little worried, but it wasn't too far to the marina on the mainland, just on the other side of our island and across the cruise ship channel.

"We gonna make it?" Dave asked.

"That's what these paddles are for, boys," I said but I knew the channel would be tough to paddle so I just prayed and got going, not wasting anymore time debating. "Hang on," I told them and throttled off around our boat and through some others trying to take the shortest route to the destination.

I was at the back controlling the motor from the left side while Sean and Dave sat together on the right and Booger crouched down and leaned on the left side over all our stuff in the front, the gas can, a water can, a backpack with soaps and clothes in case we found a real shower. We were gliding over the tropical waters in our little dinghy. It was cool the way it turned on a dime and didn't need wind to go.

"This is sick!" Dave yelled.

"Haha!" I laughed into the wind as we started picking up speed heading for the channel now. "Whaddya think, Boog?" I asked still smiling and laughing.

"Good shit," he said giving me the thumbs up, it felt like he had more to say though.

"Yeww!" Sean yelled out.

"Whoah, look at these reefs!" Dave said as we crossed over them quickly. I wanted to stop and check it out, but we needed to keep moving, they didn't know how low on gas we were.

"Yup, crazy! This is where we live now," I shouted gunning it for the channel. "Looks choppy up ahead," I yelled warning them and continued on.

As soon as we got into the channel it became clear we were a tiny boat in big boat territory. It was a lot different than being in our sailboat. We were so low and so small it was like being in a two-door car on a highway full of semi-trucks and big rigs but with a very slow engine. The smooth placid crystal-clear tropical water we were gliding through quickly turned to waves 2-3 feet high, all around choppy waters splashed us as we bounced over the waves actually getting air sometimes.

"Whoaw," Booger yelled.

"Fuuck," Dave shouted.

"Yehess," Sean screamed and I slowed it down suddenly bringing water up behind us and wetting the engine. I instantly sped it back up a little and found a speed that allowed us to ride over the waves rather than jump them. Just as I was getting a hold of it, the engine puttered one last time and pooped out.

"What happened?" Booger shouted.

"I don't know, start paddling," I ordered and simultaneously noticed the enormous cruise ship departing from its docking up the channel and heading straight for us. "PADDLE!" I yelled, grabbing the oars from the floor of the lifeboat and handed one to Sean. "Let's do this," I said and signaled with my eyes the cruise ship coming straight for us as we bobbed lifelessly. He didn't say a word and started paddling with me profusely, understanding it was no joke.

"You guys got this," Dave said, me and Sean splashed and struggled to get some momentum. Paddle after paddle of feeling like we were stuck in one spot, we started noticing we were moving again.

"You're doing it!" Dave said.

"You guys got this," Booger said.

Me and Sean didn't say a word other than grunt noises as we paddled for dear life.

"There it is," Booger yelled the most excited I'd heard him in days as the marina came into sight and we finally started to clear the raging current of the channel and waters began to mellow.

"Ugh," I stopped paddling and gasped for air exhausted from that workout.

"Haha, you good, bro?" Sean asked not looking as tired as I was but he knew that was nuts. It was more than the physical aspect.

"Shit, I thought we were gonna die," I said still trying to catch my breath. "You two take over," I said handing my paddle to Booger, the cruise ship honked as it passed.

"That thing almost ate us," Sean said laughing and continued paddling.

"Really? You think it would have hit us?" Dave asked.

"I don't know but I wasn't sticking around to find out," I said reaching for our water jug and swigged the last remaining strange tasting drops.

"Where do we go?" Booger asked.

"Not sure, mate, follow the path of boats," I said.

They continued to paddle us into this marina and we were passing very expensive ships and yachts. "Yup, keep going," I said and stood a little to try and get a better look. I could see nothing but boats and docks and many rows of it, so I picked the first one. "Down there," I said pointing and leading the way standing up as my crew of pirates paddled us to find a place to dock. It looked like just a dead end, but we could see a few other dinghies. "This is it, boys, keep paddling," I said and soon we reached a dock full of dinghies where we pulled up, got off, and tied up.

"We finally made it," I said slapping Booger on the back.

"Yes!"

"Woohoo!"

Different types of cheers came from the crew.

"Civilization," Booger said triumphantly.

"Yeah they're real civilized here on land, mate," I said and laughed, Sean and Dave did, too.

"Let's find where we pay," I said after securing the boat and started making our way down one skinny wooden dock to another in the direction of the mainland eventually coming to a shack-like shop on the dock with a sign that said, "Pay to use dinghy dock" with the rates listed.

$20 for the day

$60 for the week

$120 for the month

"Well, what do you think?" I asked looking at the guys.

"We got enough for the week pass and some gas," Booger said flatly.

"And then that's it?" I asked.

"Yeah," Booger said.

"Should we get the day and some gas and have some left for food?" I asked.

"But then if we wanna come back tomorrow it's $20 again," Booger said.

"Well, we don't have to come every day," I said.

Everyone paused to think, "But yeah, I'm good with the boat food while it lasts. Let's do the week pass if that's what we all want to do with the last of the money," I said.

"Cool," Booger said and he handed me the cash.

I took out the $60 and handed what was left back, like $10 or so.

"You guys go get the gas," I said and went into the shop and got the week-long dinghy dock pass with no problems and by the time I was back out the boys were finished getting gas and water.

"Good job, brothas," I said happily and smiling wide. They were standing there waiting with the jugs.

"Good to go," Dave said and Sean held up the giant water can with both hands over his head victoriously some dripping down onto him.

"Alrighty, let's gas up, put that stuff away, and go exploring!" I said leading them back to the dinghy with our pass which was a green sticker with the date it started and ended. "All set," I said slapping it on the front of the dinghy.

"That's it? We're good to go?" Booger asked.

"All set," I repeated, "Just cover the gas after you pour some in with that towel so no one steals it," I said.

"You think they will?" Dave asked pouring the gas and filling the tank.

"Could," I said. "But the dude inside said they keep a good eye on things," I added reassuringly.

"Let's go!" Sean shouted already ten steps down the dock.

"Let's go!" I repeated and we started jogging down the wooden docks and right out, searching for the exit.

"This way," Sean yelled from up ahead, Me and Dave were right behind him followed by Booger with the backpack flopping around with every step.

I was suddenly being lured in by the unequivocal smells of delicious fish and steak dinners wafting from the dozens of restaurants and stores that greeted us at the entrance.

"Oh God!" Dave yelled dramatically. "We need more money!"

"Haha," we all laughed.

"Yeah that smells fucking amazing," I said. We were surrounded by civilization so unexpectedly it was overwhelming. There was a public bathroom with showers that cost $1.00. We spent the last of our money there and cleaned up and changed feeling fresh and great.

"I've never felt so refreshed in my life," I said stepping out when I met the crew outside.

"Yeah, I feel brand new," Dave said.

"Where do we go?" Booger asked.

"I don't know, let's just walk and get a feel for it," I said as we continued walking past restaurants and people and stores. It felt like we were on the outside looking in, like we weren't part of it we were just moving through it as it happened all around us.

The sights and sounds of the world culture-shocking us from the silence of the sea we had just returned from. Hustle and bustle of people and cars, tourists at bars which were said to have the best drink or best lobster or to be the smallest, every place had a claim to fame and someone to sell it to. We continued block after block for a while as the initial luster wore off. We had gone from being enamored to realizing we had no money for any of this entertainment.

"Should we go back now?" Dave asked.

"I'm down," Sean said.

"Yeah, the sun will start setting soon," I said.

"What's the rush?" Booger asked seeming annoyed and it felt almost like he was trying to give me a taste of my own medicine.

"I don't know how the dinghy will be in the channel at night," I said but I was just ready to go back and eat and smoke.

"Relax, enjoy it!" Booger said mocking me from the day before.

"Ok," I said. "Let's go, lead the way," I said motioning forward with my hands and he didn't hesitate, taking off with a much lighter bag now that we were wearing the clothes from it.

Up one road and down the next we traveled further and further from the dock finally turning one last corner before I said, "Alright, let's head ba…" but I couldn't finish. I was in shock at what I was seeing. It was like an outdoor circus or something, there were people on stilts, fire-eaters, magicians, jugglers, acrobats, and food cart vendors all performing around this giant parking lot by the sea. Each with their own crowd and all with the same backdrop of the setting sun.

"Yeah, let's go back," Booger turned around and started walking past me, Sean and Dave all frozen in amazement.

"Alright, you were right," I said grabbing him as he passed.

"Haha!" Booger laughed.

"Did you know this was here?" I asked him.

"Nope, just felt like walking," Booger said.

"Good find, mate," I said like a pirate. Sean and Dave still stood staring in amazement.

"This is epic," Dave said.

"Yeah," Sean agreed still jaw dropped.

"This is it," I said.

"What?" Dave said.

"How we're gonna make money," I said, they all looked at me, even Sean managed to turn away for a moment.

"How?" Dave asked.

"Yeah, I'm not juggling fire, well maybe," Sean said.

"No dudes, our music, we'll play and they'll pay," I said making the guitar strumming motion, playing air guitar then pointing at the hundreds of tourists throwing money in hats and buckets of performers they liked.

"You think they'd pay us?" Dave asked.

"NO," Booger said.

"I know they will," I said confidently ignoring Booger.

"We don't even have any good songs," Booger said.

"We'll make more," I said, "C'mon Boog."

"Are you sure we can even join?" Dave asked.

"There's gotta be a way. I don't even think they all work together. I think it's just the spot to do it because the cruise ships come in here. This is right by where we originally pulled in when we landed here. It's a sign," I finished talking and went up to a performer with no crowd who was packing up a bunch of ropes not sure what their act was, but I was curious how to become a performer. They pointed me in the direction of a little shed-like hut with a window like a ticket booth where you could pay $5.00 for a spot but it was first come first serve, spots are dealt at 5:00 pm and had limited availability. I thanked them and grabbed the crew.

"Let's get back to the ship eh? We've got songs to write," I said and we headed back to the dinghy dock at the marina.

Along the way we saw the night life really come to life as we passed bar fights, bum fights, and neon lights. Everything blurred together as we walked now with a purpose of first finding our boat and then the purpose of getting to work! We all knew it, we needed money and honestly the peace and quiet on the boat mixed with some jams sounded nice to me after this experience of a fiery drunken circus from hell our first time back to "civilization" — it was anything but civilized which reminded me as we finally found the dock where our dinghy was, "Hopefully, no one robbed us," I blurted out. I had meant to say that in my head but I was exhausted.

"Damn yeah forgot about that," Dave said.

"We'll be alright," I said as I got into our dinghy and checked it out, "Gas is still here," I said, "So that's a good sign," and I started the engine up.

Booger, Dave, and then Sean hopped in. We weren't very talkative the entire walk ever since the new plan. I think we were all thinking and really tired. Sean untied us and I began steering us slowly out of the marina through the dark black waters of the night shimmering with reflections from dock lights like street-lights, lining the paths to rich people's boats.

I started going fast.

"Slow down," Booger said. "You're gonna disturb these people."

I let off the gas.

"True, I'm just beat," I said back and we continued crawling out making no wake as are the rules at marinas, but when we hit the channel I hit the gas.

"WOOHOO!" Sean yelled as we tore across the water. The air felt so refreshing as it blew the city smells off our skin and replaced it with ocean breeze and sea salt.

"Whoah," Booger said getting low in the boat.

"You're alright, mate," I yelled.

The water was like glass as we skated across it, reflecting the speckled lights of moon and stars ahead with the city lights behind us, suddenly accompanied by an all too familiar heart-stopping sight I didn't think even existed out here. The spots of yellow light quickly turned to red and blue as a giant engine roared up behind us and a voice called out over a loud speaker.

"This is the U.S. Coast Guard. Stop!"

I let off the gas and they pulled up next to us in a big motorized military looking boat and hit us with a spotlight.

"Driving without lights?" a man said from the deck. "We're gonna have to give you a ticket," the man said, "Go ahead and tie this to your dinghy and lead us to your boat." He tossed a big line at us and walked away.

"This is it boys," I looked at them knowing it could be my last chance to say what I needed to before we got arrested. "Hey, we had fun, right?"

"Once in a lifetime man," Dave said.

Booger looked scared.

Sean looked clueless.

I whispered, "If they go onto our boat, we are fucked."

Everyone was suddenly on the same page and we all made that face where you tuck your lips in and try and smile through the sadness but we knew the jig was up.

"Ok let's go," the Coast Guard yelled and I leaned back and started motoring again, slowing leading my crew to doom. It looked like we were towing this giant boat with our dinghy through the night as we came upon our ship.

"This is it here," I yelled and pulled up to it. "Pull us in Sean," I said gloomily and he grabbed our boat, tying us up while I shut off the engine.

"Registration and identification," the man said as they slowly got closer and tied onto our sailboat.

"Yes, one moment, it's inside," I said leaving the boys scared shitless on deck.

I popped back out with the paperwork and my ID handing it to the man promptly. It was all beat up and tattered as he unfolded it and inspected the information. My heart was pounding as I tried to keep it together but the whole time I was thinking, "Please don't come on my boat. Please don't smell weed. Please. Please. Please. God help!"

Weed was still not legal after everything the movement had been through. It was still somehow criminal to have this healing herb that was more harmful to your wallet or your fridge than a human. In fact, I was worried they might even try and hit us with distribution. We had at least a half pound still. They could arrest us and take our boat, but not our story.

I smiled at the man and nodded as he wrote something down.

"Ok, here's your ticket," he said, handing it to me along with the other paperwork and my ID back.

"You have 180 days to pay the fine or prove you fixed the problem," the man said.

"How do I fix the problem?" I said trying to play along when I should have just said okay goodbye.

"You carry a red light with you at night on your dinghy," he said.

"How do I prove it?" I asked like an idiot, I felt a nudge from Booger.

"It's all in the paperwork and online," he said sounding over it as well.

"K, thank you so much," I said. "And we're good to keep using the dinghy," I asked.

"You want me to come over there and read it for you sir?" the Coast Guard asked shining the spotlight directly on my face.

"No, no, sorry, thank you," I said.

"All set, have a good night," he said with a nonchalant salute and they were gone.

"Huh huh huh holy shit dude!" Sean gasped with excitement celebrating.

I sat down or my legs gave out and the bench caught me, as I breathed for the first time in ten minutes staring at the ground and then looked up, took a deep breath in and stood up, "Blunt time," I said.

"Are you serious?" Booger asked and Sean and Dave cheered.

"Smoke it while you got it," I said.

"Yeah, they coulda just took it all and took us to jail," Dave said.

"I know but shouldn't we figure something out about the ticket?" Booger asked and maybe he was right, but I was over and done with it.

"You heard the man, 180 days," I said putting my arm around Booger and pulling him in awkwardly close, "Now let's make some music and smoke some weed in paradise," I said letting him go and slapped him on the back, but he looked less than amused.

"Whatever you say bro," Booger said.

"That's the spirit," I said and went down to roll a blunt, "Last blunt and we forgot papers," I yelled.

I felt reinvigorated, one thing after another, from finding the dinghy dock to dealing with water cops, I felt like we couldn't be stopped. We had been to hell and back today and deserved to party.

Sean and Dave were making drinks, Booger started cooking some late night rice and I was rolling up, thinking about what new songs to make for the tourists. We went on with our night like nothing ever happened in fact I think we all felt a little better about finally facing one of our biggest fears, the Coast Guard and making it out generally unscathed. I know I at least wasn't gonna let bureaucratic bullshit rain on my parade, not tonight, not ever.

Again we smoked, drank, and lived like humble kings as we partied and jammed in paradise. Food, water, shelter, great views and everything we needed for less than it cost to live normally with daily fast food and excess impulse buys.

Day 15

That night I fell asleep knowing we had made the right decision to take this journey, which is why I was so surprised when I woke up to find Booger was not so sure he should have come. He was on the deck using one of the cell phones talking in code. I knew it was the phone because I could see Sean and Dave asleep still on the benches. I could tell it wasn't good from the tone. I could hear him clearly because he was on the bow and I had slept on the front V-bed area, the triangle spot. He sounded serious but quiet like his captors were in the next room and he must finish before they found him.

"NO," he said in a low tone.

"NO," he said again.

"NOW," he said.

I got up and started moving around pretending I didn't hear him. He must have hung up fast because he came into the cabin before I made it out to the deck.

"Oy me boy, how ye be?" I asked in a pirate voice loudly waking the boys and smiling at him, curious to hear what he had to say.

"Good, mate yar," he said replying in a pirate voice and walking past me to prepare a bowl of granola or something.

"Good to hear 'cause we've got work to do today," I said picking up my pipe guitar.

"Wake N' Bake," Sean who must have been listening sprung up and shouted joyfully.

"Give me a few more minutes," Dave said rolling back over.

"Let's go we got no time to waste," I said. "Oh I like that, could be a new one right there," I added excited and took a hit from the boot bowl in the guitar pipe left over from last night's jam, then strummed it.

> Time to go no time to waste
>
> Thank you for that little taste

I sang out a little random verse and played the guitar.

"That was sick actually," Dave said and rolled back over, facing us.

"Right let's let them know we might not be here long," I said excited that he liked it too, "And then we thank them for the money they just gave us before they do it, or it could be while they're dropping cash in," I said and made up some more continuing to play the guitar.

> Thanks for your time and your money
>
> Thanks for your fine little honey

I stopped playing, swigged some honey, and laughed, "They'll have to throw money in."

"Ok Ok, I'm up," Dave said.

"Yeah c'mon let's go guys, we better get started if we wanna perform tonight!" I said.

"What!? No way!" Booger boogered.

"Why not?" I asked.

"We've got nothing to play," he said.

"What about that Bobbin' song?" Dave said.

"Yeah I liked that one," Sean said.

"That's one," Booger said.

"And I just made one up," I said.

"That's two," Booger said, "if you count that."

"We can do covers," Sean said smoking a bowl now out on the deck. I followed him out there with the guitar and the bag full of weed.

"Yeah, we can do covers if we need to fill gaps," I said.

"I don't think we're ready," Booger said.

"Well we better get ready fast, we only have a week to make more money," I said.

"Let's practice the Bobbin' song and your new one today and see how we feel tonight," Dave said trying to settle the difference.

"Word, I bet we can get it down good enough for tonight and maybe make a few bucks!" I said.

"Doubt it, but ok," Booger said agreeing.

We sat there for most of the day practicing, other than eating and smoking, we were playing and singing. I actually needed more breaks than them for my vocal chords. But as the sun went down, I too knew we weren't ready and it wasn't worth the gas we would use to get there, but I did come up with another song we all knew was perfect.

The sun was setting and the show began. The most brilliant hues of yellows and reds mixed and blended, creating perfect tonal fades from orange to pink, as we wondered at its greatness, I realized so obviously that that's what they were here to do, every evening over there thousands of tourists come to watch the sun go down. So, we wrote a song about just that and it went like this:

The Sun is going down

I said the Sun is going dooown

It's just another day in paradise

I said it feels so great

Gotta say it twice

The Sun is going down

I said the sun is goin dooown

"It's gotta be repetitive man, that part's so good I want them to hear it even if they only walk by for a split second," I said. We all loved it and practiced for a little longer, then called it a night.

DAY 16

The Sun came up and we now had three songs. We practiced again on and off all day getting ready to perform on land. I was so anxious, the day flew by, I found myself a few times saying, "We gotta be there by five!" and before I knew it Sean was saying, "Cheers! Happy 4:20."

"Four Twenty!" I yelled, "We gotta go!"

"Na, we're gonna miss it," Booger said.

"No the fuck we're not. Get in the boat!" I said starting to put things away quickly, fumbling my lighter and scurrying to hide the weed.

"Let's go, grab the instruments!" I shouted and jumped into the dinghy firing her up and revving it like a stock car.

"Yeww!" Sean yelled jumping around still on the boat.

"Let's Go, Let's Go!" I yelled and Dave jumped in, Booger was trailing behind, "Lock it up!" I yelled one last thing and he was in.

I took off speeding towards the marina, which took like ten minutes, then like 20-30 jogging to the lot where we needed to reserve the spot by 5:00pm. Cutting it close was an understatement but I figured it's an island, they'd be lenient. Four Fifty Eight pm and we were turning onto the street where the performances happened, another turn and there, around the corner was the little make-shift ticket window. The person was closing it up and pulling down a curtain over the window.

"NOO!" I yelled sprinting to the window, "Please, don't close," I begged.

The person paused, and I held out our last Five dollars in the world. They took it and assigned us a spot. We were in.

"Thank you!" I said and turned to the boys, "You guys ready to make some money!?"

"Hope so, that was our last five bucks," Booger said.

"Well then it would have been gone soon anyway, I just invested it," I said smiling, deflecting his negative energy, I had faith in us.

"I'm ready," Dave said.

"Yup, me too," Sean said.

"Then let's fucking do this," I said and led them to where the spot vendor assigned us according to the paper print-out map of the lot.

"Wow, this is sick!" I said walking up to our designated performance spot on the ocean side of the lot, right on the water.

"How'd we get this awesome spot?" Dave asked.

"That's crazy," Sean said.

"Are you sure?" Booger asked realizing it was a great spot too.

All the tourists coming off the cruise ships would have to walk right passed us.

"Says so right here mate," I said pointing to the paper. "Let's claim the spot and practice a little but save ourselves for the big crowd," I said.

It was still early and the lot was pretty empty, but I started getting nervous. What if no one liked us and I just wasted our last dollars or what if no one even shows up? I was trying to play it cool, but I was worried I had just fucked up. An hour had gone by and no crowds came.

"I'll be back," Booger said and put his guitar down, walking off. I didn't even say anything.

"Yeah I'm going to check out the dude with the coconuts," Dave said and put the pipe guitar down.

"Aw c'mon guys, it's gunna start soon, I'm tellin' ya," I shouted as Dave walked off. "Go ahead," I said to Sean. I knew he wanted to explore too, and he took off, leaving me to wonder if I had made the right choice. I found myself second guessing a lot of my recent decisions as resources started to dwindle.

"Here ya go," Dave said interrupting my downer moment and handed me a coconut with the top cut off. It was full of coconut milk and meat.

"How'd you get this?" I said exasperated by the surprise.

"He gave them to us FREE!" Dave yelled, "I told him about our band and he hooked it up."

I looked over at the coconut dude who caught me looking and waved at us with a giant machete smiling. I waved back, "Thank You!" I yelled and then drank the juice, tilting it back and chugged it like alcohol. Just then a fog horn blasted and a ship pulled up right on time as the sunset show commenced with Mother Nature as the headlining act but we were a strong opener I believed as people started flocking off the cruise ship in droves, visiting each performance along the way.

"Where's Booger?" I asked ready to get started.

"Don't know," Dave said as Sean rejoined us.

"Fuck!" I said and he emerged from the crowd, "Oh thank God! Where'd you go?" I asked.

"Bathroom," Booger said.

"Alright, alright. You good?" I said and looked at them all, they nodded, "Let's start with Bobbin'," I said and counted them off, "1,2,1,2,3,4."

We had one of the guitar cases open in front of us to be our oversized tip jar. I saw a dollar go in then another as more people unloaded off the ships. We continued playing but looked at each other and smiled when the money went in and we started interrupting our own songs to say thank you. A couple of people stopped and stayed listening, then a few, then several, and the money followed suit. The guitar case was filling up nicely. People were loving the songs especially the sunset song. I saw a five dollar bill go in during that one, I knew we could do it.

It was perfect. It was like clockwork. Every three songs a new group came in and we always ended with the sunset song keeping the same order. I think we played each song three or four times with practically no breaks. We didn't want to miss a dime. But as the sun actually finally went down, the crowd died down too, and it was a good thing because my raspy voice was at max rasp and it needed a break and some honey. I like chugging honey straight from the bottle after a long night of jamming it always soothes the throat.

"Well that worked," Dave said squatting down next to the open guitar case and shuffling it around with his hand.

"Dudes, we killed it!" I said. "Look at all this!" I got down with Dave by the case.

"There's five's in here!" Sean yelled getting down with us, but Booger was just picking up his stuff less than impressed. He came from money.

"Dude you killed it, Boog!" I said to him, trying to hype him up but it didn't work.

"Nice, can we get some food," he said sounding mad but I ignored it, he's a weirdo.

"YES!" Sean yelled. "Burgers."

"Haha yeah of course. We got money now," I said and closed the guitar case with the money still in it.

The case was all lined with like a red faux fur or something, it looked nice.

"Shouldn't we take the money out?" Booger asked noticing what I just did.

"I don't know, I thought we'd keep our business papers in the brief case," I said jokingly.

Sean and Dave started cracking up.

"Nice, yes," Dave said.

"Then what are you going to do with the guitar?" Booger asked but he looked like he regretted asking.

"We'll keep it out and play as we walk, maybe get more money," I said smiling.

"Alright whatever let's just go," Booger said and we made our way back to the main street with all the stores and bars and restaurants. I was carrying the guitar case and Dave was noodling the guitar while we walked.

"Where do we start?" Dave asked.

"I don't know, let's just walk 'til you see something you want to eat," I replied.

"How much money did we even make?" Booger asked shortly.

"I saw some 5's," Sean said.

"So we got at least 10," I said.

"And a bunch of ones," Dave added in.

"I bet like 17 dollars," I said proudly, "Not bad for our first time," I added.

"That's barely enough," Booger said.

"Well, we'll do it again tomorrow and the next day and the next day and it will add up, or at least keep us full and happy," I said trying to keep on that high.

"What about weed? When we run out?" Booger said.

"We'll find a square grouper. I don't know man, do we have to do this now?" I said.

"Hot dogs!" Sean yelled. "Burgers!" he yelled again.

We had come to a food vendor on the street. A hot dog stand but it wasn't hot dogs. It was hamburgers in the shape of hot dogs.

"Burger dogs!" she yelled. "They're burger dogs."

"What the heck is a burger dog?" Sean hollered.

"Exactly how it sounds, son, burger shaped like a hot dog," the lady answered him. She was like an old biker chick with short hair and a leather jacket even though it was hot as balls out.

"You boys hungry?" she asked in her rough tone.

"Starving," I said stepping up with the case full of money still closed.

"You boys play?" she asked.

"Yeah," I said.

"Let me hear ya," she said and we played Bobbin. She laughed and said, "You boys play your music here for me and I'll feed you."

"OK," Sean yelled grabbing a burger dog she was holding and offering as part of the deal.

"Shoot, my voice is shit from performing tonight," I said.

"Well, you promise to come back tomorrow?" she asked.

I thought for a moment and realized we only needed money for food right now so this was a perfect deal and maybe we could still do both.

"Yeah, I'm down, that actually sounds amazing," I said grabbing a burger dog, too. "Thank you so much," I said and the boys all grabbed one and thanked her.

"Now I wanna see you back here, same time tomorrow, y'all," she said seriously, "Brings in more customers when there's live music," she added.

"Yeah, that makes total sense, we'll definitely be here! Thanks again," I said genuinely thankful and excited. "What a night. We got paid, got fed, and had a great time doing it, that's what life is all about," I said cheerfully as we walked home eating our burger dogs.

"These are fucking godly," Dave said.

"Yeah yub muking fo good," Sean said stuffing his last bite in his mouth.

Me and Dave laughed but I couldn't help but notice the dark cloud floating with us and it wasn't weather.

"Booger, dude, what's the problem?" I asked.

"This thing's gross and I'm fucking hungry," he said.

"Really!?" Sean exclaimed but I wasn't surprised.

"Well, we got plenty of money, get whatever you want, we are all full," I said starting to get upset but really trying not to ruin the killer night we just had on this once in a lifetime epic voyage.

"There's nothing I like around here," Booger said.

"I don't know what to tell you man I'm sorry," I said.

"Yeah me too," he said under his breath and we made our way to the dinghy dock.

I let out a big sigh, it had gotten to me even though I tried so hard not to let it, but his energy was infectious. We walked in silence 'til we were at the dinghy.

"Everybody in? Good," I said starting the engine and quickly pulling out with no warning.

"Whoah," Booger said.

"Yeah, hold on," I said barely under my breath angrily and floored it home to our sailboat.

Sean tied us up like usual and I went to bed. I was pissed off and holding back potential energy that was meant to punch somebody. I was mad that I was mad because we should be celebrating and Booger just snotted all over it. I was mad I let him do it.

"Night man," Sean said as he packed a bowl or something.

"Night brother," I said and passed out.

Day 17

I woke up in a pool of sweat. It was getting hotter every day. The sun was up and so was the crew cooking, smoking, and practicing already.

"Mornin' boys," I said and jumped off the side of the boat splashing into the water.

"AAY," Sean said and jumped in after me.

"Oh that feels nice," I said treading water and splashing some in my face.

"Yeah, it's fucking hot out," Sean said.

"I think that's why I got up so early," Dave said from the boat talking to us as he played and smoked the guitar pipe.

Booger was cooking rice and didn't say much. I figured it was just going to go on the rest of the trip, so I needed to just ignore him unless he needed help or wanted to join in.

"Good thing we are surrounded by beautiful water," I said.

"Yeah and those showers are clutch at the marina," Dave said.

Me and Sean climbed back up onto the boat and took a seat on the benches, drying off in the hot sun and smoking but as soon as we dried off we were wet with sweat.

"Damn, it's hot," Sean said.

"Let's practice huh? Maybe get our mind off this heat," I said.

"Yeah," they all said except Booger.

"Practice?" he said, "I'm dying guys."

"C'mon Boog, we're all hot but," Dave started to say but Booger cut him off.

"I'm bored," Booger said.

"What do you mean? You're bored?" I couldn't hold it back. "We're in paradise. Relax, float around, make a drink, write a song, there's a million things you can do. You should be thankful for the million things you don't have to be doing," I finished and walked away to pack a bowl.

"Yeah, you gotta just chill man. Try and take it all in," Dave said. I heard him trying to console Booger, but I was done.

"I'm trying," Booger said grabbing the surfboard and a pair of sunglasses and his floppy hat, he took his shirt off and went to the back of the boat and climbed down the little ladder into the water slowly and tied the board by its leash to the boat.

"What are you doin?" I heard Sean say. "There's no waves," he laughed joking with Booger, but Booger ignored him and laid back on the board looking up at the sky. It was clear now he was just floating.

"Haha nice," Sean said.

Booger gave him a thumbs up but kept staring at the sky. Somehow he still looked like a tourist in the group after all that we did, he still had that look.

I was now smoking on the deck watching and smiling just glad to see him finally enjoying the ride it seemed. I ate some food and smoked waiting 'til Booger came back to the boat. We were running low on canned chicken and tuna pretty much everything which reminded me…

"Hey you guys wanna practice for tonight?" I asked them all as we roasted on the deck.

"Yeah, let's do it," Sean said grabbing the bongo drum.

"Meh," Booger said.

"Come on Booger dude, let's jam," Dave said.

I rolled my eyes.

"We told that lady we'd play for her tonight at her food stand, too," I said.

"Burger dogs!" Sean and Dave yelled simultaneously.

"Blah," Booger said making a puking noise.

"Haha well we gotta," I said.

"Alright whatever," Booger said.

"Man we just need to make some more money plus it's fun I think anyway," I said.

"Hell yeah," Sean said.

"Yeah I'm enjoying it," Dave said followed by an awkward silence.

"Let's just burn and practice and get over there, kill it again tonight, and we'll make more for gas, showers, and real food, plus weed, when we run out," I said.

"If we don't find some," Sean said excitedly.

"We're not going to find any," Booger said, "But alright, let's jam."

So we jammed and practiced for the night's sunset show and after party performance at the burger dog joint. The songs became tighter and we were sounding more confident that what we were playing was good. We had already got money for it as confirmation along with the reactions of passersby and they were from all over the world. I started to think maybe we could even make a name for ourselves, but we didn't even have a name yet.

"How about the Seaweed Pirates like Sean said? For our band name," I suggested.

"YES!" Sean and Dave said.

"That's dumb," Booger said, but majority rules so that was it. We had called ourselves a bunch of names but never settled on one for longer than a month.

It was 3:50 pm and we needed to be there by 5:00 pm.

"It's getting close to that time bruddas. Prepare to go to land," I said tapping out the pipe I was smoking into my hand and then blowing it into thin air.

We grabbed our shit and took off headed for the dinghy dock. We still had plenty of days on the pass. We were going around our island

and for like the third time this beautiful boat caught my eye. It was an all wooden catamaran that looked like it was built by native tribes' people, it just had that tribal vibe. You could tell it was lashed together by ropes but professionally and nicely done. This time though there was a dude on it and he had dreads.

"Ahoy!" I yelled and threw up the hang ten sign with my hand as we passed him, and he waved back.

"That's cool," I said to the boys, "Another dready, maybe he smokes."

"Yeah probably!" Dave said and we continued to the marina and then quickly onto the ticket booth to get a spot to perform.

We were running late again but managed to snag a spot. I even wrote our new name inside the guitar case so when it was open for tips it clearly read "The Seaweed Pirates." When we got to our spot and started setting up and getting ready to rock even harder than the night before, a dude walked up to us…

"Hello there, friends," he said sounding professional but looking like he was from the streets or maybe a sailor like us.

"Hey," we all said basically just acknowledging him slightly as we continued talking and making our little area look good setting out the guitar case and a baja blanket to sit on, but he wasn't done.

"I'm Mr. Jimmy, your new manager," he was holding a wooden stool and put it down in the area we set up. "My last band just left me today, you're in luck!"

"Uuh," we all kind of said and stared at him. He wasn't much older than us.

"Uh, Mr. Jimmy," I said starting to talk to him like he might be slow. I didn't want to upset him but we were all set.

"Yes," he said smiling.

"We don't need a manager, but thank you," I said politely rejecting him but Sean sat on the stool.

"Well, he's sitting on the stool, and whoever sits on the stool is who I manage," he said still smiling.

I suddenly felt like I knew what was happening here, he wanted a cut of whatever we made and was offering the stool as his part of the gig.

"Oh, we're all set," I said ripping it out from under Sean who was just entertained by the conversation and shoved it into Mr. Jimmy's arms. "Here's your stool, thanks for the offer," I said.

"You're nothing without me kid!" he said angrily stomping off sounding like he was living a delusional Hollywood dream.

I just looked back at the boys and laughed… "Ok then who's ready to rock?" I said and we did for the next four hours or so, we fucking rocked. It looked like twice the money went into the case and I had the bottle of honey with me keeping my throat going strong. I had to sing later at the burger dog place which was good and bad because I was starving but not sure if my vocals would hold up.

The sun went down and we made a beeline for the food stand.

"Fellas!" she yelled standing there happy to see us and had a burger dog in each hand.

"Hey," we all yelled back and took the food she was handing us.

"Go ahead and set up right there, you can play all night if you want, but when I tell you to move it, ya gotta go" She said.

"Go where?" I asked, confused.

"At least around the block and then come back," she said.

"Why are we doing that?" Booger spoke up.

"The cops walk around here and bust you if you don't have a permit, and I didn't think y'all had permits," she said.

"Oh, shoot okay," I said, "Nice thank you."

"Thank you," Sean and Dave said.

"You're more than welcome, like I said, live music really brings the crowd around here, hey I'm Rhonda by the way," she said putting her hand out to shake.

"Joe," I said and shook her hand, but she pulled me in for a big bear hug and let me go.

"K Joe and friends go ahead and bring me some customers," she said smiling and went back to cooking burger meat.

"We're going by the name The Seaweed Pirates," I said in a pirate voice, "Yarr."

"Then bring me some booties," she said and we all laughed.

Me, Sean and Dave scarfed down the dogs and got into position with our guitar case open next to a tree in the sidewalk in front of the food stand. Booger was there, too, I appreciated him playing here with us even though he wasn't eating anything, but we could maybe make more money, too.

"Ready dudes?" I said.

"Yarr," they said back mocking me and we all laughed and then started jamming and sure enough the people followed the sound right to us, and the food.

There was a long line forming and while they waited, they tossed money into our case. The dollars went in and we played on, we played our few originals and some covers and before we knew it a couple hours had gone by and we were beat. The case was full of crumpled ones and random 5's. It was unreal just doing what we loved and getting paid.

"Man, my throat's done," I sounded like someone lost in the desert and badly in need of water, with my raspy voice.

"Yeah, my fingers could use a break," Dave said.

"Ready when you are," Sean said.

We looked at Booger…

"Oh I've been ready to leave," he said, but he didn't sound mad or anything.

"Cool," I said rubbing my throat and closed up the guitar case.

Besides the money, I feel like we had really been getting our new name out there with the sign and strangers who would ask. We were the Seaweed Pirates and everyone would know it soon.

"Thanks Rhonda!" I yelled. She still had a couple customers, so I didn't want to bother her, but she yelled back.

"See ya tomorrow Seaweed Pirates!"

We walked back in silence. It had become our usual thing walking together, exhausted after long days of jamming and island lifestyle, down dark quiet back streets that led to the marina.

"That was pretty cool," Booger said. We all looked at him at the same time shocked he was even talking and that it was positive for once lately.

"Cha ha," Sean said.

"That was sick," Dave said joining in. It was all coming out at once.

"Yeah I think they like the name and our songs, shit I think they like us," I said laughing.

"So wild," Booger said like he hadn't believed it 'til now.

"Yeah man I'm glad we did this," I said.

"Yeah me too," Dave said, "It's definitely epic."

"Yeah," Sean said.

"Yeah," Booger said, and we all let out a sigh of some sort and continued walking down the island alleys quietly thinking 'til we got to the marina.

The air seemed different that night. It was almost hollow with uncertainty, still with silence but unlike the other muted nights this night was eerie as we got into the dinghy and slowly cruised through the marina.

"A real pirate night," I said in my pirate voice breaking the silence and a vocal chord it felt like as I strained my voice to be funny.

"Yeah creepy," Dave said.

There was a light mist in the air, like a tropical storm was forming from the heat of the day mixing with the relative coolness of the night and the waters. It was the perfect recipe for a storm. We made it home to our ship just in time as lightning cracked through the sky and raindrops started falling.

"Hoho!" Sean yelled as we all dove into the cabin to avoid being struck.

"Yo that was close!" Dave said.

"Haha," I laughed. "We're fine," I said but I was aware of the danger, no need to worry us though because what could we do now anyway, but Booger was bugging.

"No this could be bad," he said sounding panicked.

"It's all good, man we're inside," Dave said.

"I saw stuff about masts being like lightning rods, before we left, I checked into it guys. It's possible," Booger said.

"Well, what do ya want to do? Dinghy back to the mainland," I asked sarcastically because that would obviously be dumb it was pouring raining, and thundering and lightning.

"No, there's a full-on storm out there. I'm just worried," Booger said.

"Well, don't be," I said. "I think in this case size matters and we don't have the biggest rod in the yard, Boog," I said laughing, which was true, there were bigger sailboats right next to us with bigger masts than our own. He looked relieved by my joke at least for the moment so I took advantage of that to change the subject.

"Dudes we absolutely annihilated it again. Let's smoke!" I said as the boat began to really rock.

"Yes!" said Sean.

"Haha yeah," Dave said.

A loud thunder boomed and the boat's never-ending motion increased as the waters stirred. There was definitely a bad storm upon us but there was really nothing we could do but batten down the hatches and burn 'til it blew over. I was freaked out, too. I had seen the videos of masts struck by lightning and blasting holes in hulls like they were papier mache. But I knew however I reacted to the situation, would set the tone for the rest of the crew. So, I laughed it off and we smoked inside with the hatches closed, completely fish-bowling the cabin and I don't remember much more before we went to sleep other than Sean saying, "'Cause when we see weed, we smoke it!" and we all laughed. It felt like things were finally coming together for us all.

Day 18

"We must have been alright,

Because we made it through the night,

And I woke to see another morning light."

I thought to myself but kind of said it under my breath as I got up freestyling on what could be a new song. I was in a good mood. The sun was coming up and I was feeling great about the band.

"Morning bruddas! Rise and shine!" I said joyfully and went and picked up a pipe and packed a fresh bowl and noticed we actually were getting low on herbs.

"Damn gettin' low on weed," I said.

Sean jolted out of the hammock next to me but got hung up and ended up flopping onto the floor of the boat with a thud.

"Awhuhuh," he groaned, "Nooo worst way to wake up ever," he said having the complete opposite experience I was having. "Damn dude, haha," I said laughing, "We're not out, just down to a couple ounces. We might have to slow up 'til we find a connect," I said taking a hit and blowing it at him as I put out a hand and helped him up, then passed the pipe to him.

"Cheers," I said.

"Cheers," he said rubbing his bruised tail bone and taking a hit.

"Bring it out here," I said to Sean trying to let Booger and Dave sleep longer since they didn't want to get up obviously. We went out on the deck but everything was wet from the storm. The seat cushions were soaked.

"Damn, it stormed pretty bad last night, huh?" I said.

"Oh yeah I forgot," Sean said.

"Yeah, I fell asleep fast, slept right through it," I said.

"Same," he said as we stood at the helm passing the pipe. Then we walked up to the bow and looked at the island we were anchored at and continued to smoke.

"So crazy," I said, "Man, we are doing some shit," I hit the pipe and looked at him passing it to him.

"Yeah," he said. He was a man of few words but when he said something he meant it.

He took the pipe and finished it off with one big fat rip.

"Check this out," I said and leaned down to surprise Booger who was sleeping under us in the triangle bed thing. I opened the hatch we were standing around and poked my head down.

"Ahoy mate!" I yelled in and saw Booger sitting up texting on his phone and he didn't look happy. "Oh sorry bro, haha," I said and retreated not wanting to upset him or interrupt him.

"It's okay man but I need to talk to everyone," he said up to me through the hatch.

"Oh, okay be right there," I said and shut the hatch. Me and Sean went back to the deck and into the cabin right away. I slapped Dave's foot that was hanging off the bench a couple times.

"Ay ay, wake up," I said, he started moving. "Booger wants to talk to us, all," I added and he sat up on his bench and rubbed his eyes still half asleep.

Just then Booger came out from the V-hull looking like he had bad news and his phone still in one hand down by his side. I thought maybe someone close to him had died but didn't know what to say and it seemed he didn't either as he approached us slowly and sat down on the bench across from us all.

"Guys," he said in a low tone with his head down then looked up at us. I untied the hammock and moved it so we could all see each other without obstruction.

"What's up Booger dude? Everything okay?" I said trying to help but clearly everything was not okay.

He started to tear up and sniffled then wiped his nose.

"Guys," he said trying again. "I can't do this," and he started crying.

I didn't know what to say, it wasn't a dead family member or something but obviously he was struggling. Sean looked shocked to see our friend crying and me and Dave glanced at each other like, what do we do? And what does this mean for us?

"You're okay man, it's all good," I said trying to console him.

"No I'm not, I can't do this anymore," he cried again.

I was taken aback, in my mind this was paradise and heaven on earth, but to him it was the opposite. I couldn't understand how, why, what but it didn't matter, his mind was made up.

"Ok man well we just want you to be happy. Do what you gotta do," Dave said.

"But what about you guys?" he cried like he cared but I didn't think it mattered to him, either way he was leaving.

"We'll be alright man," I said and he cried more. We all leaned in and patted him on the back.

"It's all good man," Sean said.

"I'm sorry guys," Booger said and stood up and hugged us. "Thank you for understanding," he said.

"Yeah, no problem brother," I said trying to smile. "So what do you want to do?" I asked Booger.

"I'm going to pack up I guess. And when you go over today to jam, my parents are coming to pick me up," he said.

"Yeah I don't think we'll be jamming today without you," I said correcting him, "But I'll take you over there whenever you want," I added making the disappointed face and grabbed the weed and pipe and went out to the deck.

I took a deep breath and looked around at the new life we had created for ourselves. I was sad about Booger but worried about us, me and the remaining crew. Would I be able to navigate safely still through the night? How would it affect our sleep rotation? And would Sean and Dave be able to do whatever Booger was doing? Cooking and putting the main sail away neatly and gently? All these questions flew through my mind like a whirlwind overwhelming me, I sat down and packed a bowl. The seats were dryer but still wet, I didn't care. Sean and Dave were consoling him but I didn't care about him anymore, he was gone in my mind, man overboard, I had to take care of the rest now.

Sean came out, then Dave, they looked disheartened like they thought it was all over which triggered something in me, like a fire starting to catch fast.

"Cheer up boys, we'll be alright," I said punching Sean in the shoulder. He rubbed the spot and looked at me with a long face.

"I don't know man," he said and sat down with me.

"Yeah this will all be a lot harder with one less man," Dave said.

"Oh c'mon guys, not you too," I said forgetting Booger could hear me but I honestly didn't care if he did, "We can do this, we still can jam, it might not be as fancy but we can jam and we can sail. They say this type of boat is built to be crewed by one man if it has to be, that's why all lines lead to the helm," I finished, hit the pipe, and stood up with my new energy. "I'm gonna get ready," I said and went to change.

"Hey man, I'm really sorry," Booger said to me when I got into the cabin.

"No worries man, you gotta do what's right for you and we will be fine," I said reassuring him and myself.

"You think we can go over early today? My ride will be here around noon," he said squinching his face, he knew he was being a pain but…

"Sure, no prob brudda," I said and changed into a mixture of dirty clothes that seemed maybe less dirty.

We had washed them in a bucket once and it was getting to be that time again soon I realized as I shook the crust out of the fabric. It was almost 11:00 AM already somehow.

"Alright boys get ready! We're going to shore early today!" I yelled out to Sean and Dave.

"I'm sorry, man, is that okay?" Booger and I were talking more than we had the whole trip.

"Yeah, that's fine man," I said smiling now for real.

I was actually happy. It was time for a change and maybe this was it. I finished grabbing stuff I needed, wallet, lighter, spare pick, and headed back out onto the deck. Sean and Dave ran past me to get ready real quick grabbing the instruments and taking a few more tokes.

I got into the dinghy, checked the gas and called for the crew.

"Let's go," I shouted.

Booger came bouncing out the door of the cabin with a fat backpack and some other stuff in his hands, pillow and like his toiletries or something in a little clear bag with a toothbrush and deodorant, shit like that. He got in eager to leave.

"Ya ready, mate?" I asked. "Got everything?"

"Yessiry," he said trying to hold back his excitement, but it was obvious he couldn't wait to get home.

"Nice man," I said, "Let's go dudes and grab the instruments and red light," I yelled as they came out onto the deck.

"Gott 'em," Sean yelled.

"Lock it up good," I said.

"K, all good," Dave said and they boarded the dinghy. It was no big deal anymore to go to and from land.

"Everyone in?" I asked.

"Yep," they all said and I took off headed for shore.

We saw the dread dude again and waved but there was no time to stop. It was surreal we were about to lose a man but the whole thing had been surreal since 4/20 and honestly I never thought he was going to come. We pulled up to the dinghy dock and did our usual thing tying up and grabbing our stuff but this time Booger wouldn't be back.

"This is weird," I said, "You sure you want to leave?"

Booger looked at me quick, "Yeah man I'm done," he said and we all walked to the main entrance of the marina on the street.

"You good man?" I asked Booger.

"Aren't we waiting here with him?" Dave asked.

"I'm good," Booger said.

"Who knows how long it will take with traffic, I'm hungry, we gotta pay for our spot and I want to see what else is going on around here," I said naming off a laundry list of reasons why I didn't want to stand in the hot sun waiting for someone to leave my crew.

"Aw, man you sure?" Sean asked Booger.

"Yeah," Booger said.

"He's fine guys," I laughed trying to keep it light. It was no big deal really if anything, he was about to go to a spa compared to us. They hugged, I high fived him and said, "Was fun brother. We'll hit you up when we find Sensemilla Island."

"Haha yar right," he said in his pirate voice and we left him there.

We were quiet as we walked down the road to Main Street. We hadn't seen it at this time of day. It wasn't creepy at all, in fact it was really nice. The buildings had a unique island architecture and all the yards were full of colorful tropical flowers and fruit trees.

"Dang this is beautiful," I said maybe sounding too cheery for the guys who looked down in the dumps while I was riding on cloud-nine. They just looked at me making sad faces like they couldn't talk 'cause they might cry.

"Dudes don't let that get you down. We are still in paradise and who knows for how long. If we run outta money or something, we'll be right there with him, back at home," I said and clapped my hands together like wake up! They were taking this sea life thing too seriously like we'd never see him again.

"That's true," Sean said. I started to see the sadness leave his face.

"But I'm not that good at guitar," Dave said.

"Oh shut up bro, you're great! All we need is you on the rhythm guitar and Sean on the drum," I said and they both looked happier.

We continued walking our normal route and stopped to get some real food. While we were eating, I saw a little sign in a little window of a small business attached to the other businesses around it. It read, "Island Radio" and it piqued my interest giving me an idea and since everything was so crazy lately I figured why not?

"Let's get on the radio," I said and pointed to it.

"The radio? No way," Dave said.

"Ok Booger," I said sarcastically maybe too soon and laughed.

"I'm down," Sean said.

"Of course I'm down, I just don't think they'll let us on," Dave said.

"Well, let's see," I said and led them over to it and walked in.

Sean and Dave looked at me and then followed.

"Oh, well, hello, um how may I help you?" an elderly woman attending a front desk greeted us, startled by our sudden entrance and perhaps our appearance.

"Hello there," I said trying not to sound like a pirate but I felt like it did. "We are a band of musical sailors traveling around and playing our songs shore to shore and we'd like to play on the radio. Who do we speak with for that?" I said laying it all out there while Sean and Dave stood at my side, instruments in hand.

"Uh, well, um," she stuttered and began pointing at a man in a room behind a glass door who looked to be DJ-ing with his headset on and talking into a mic. This all happened in milliseconds. The man caught her pointing and appeared to end what he was doing on the mic, maybe to see what the commotion was. "That man can help you," she said but I was way ahead of her walking up to his door.

It swung open, "What's this?" he said looking genuinely intrigued and since what I said worked on the first lady, I repeated it verbatim to him minus the "who do we speak with" part.

"Ohkay, that's cool. Come on in," he said.

I was shocked and so were the boys. It was working and we just kept going with it. Maybe he was bored maybe he was scared I don't know. We went in with him and he directed us towards some stools on the other side of his DJ-ing area where he had sound boards and computers, the works.

"Ok what's the name of your band?" he asked flicking buttons and putting his headset on.

This was happening and it was happening right now. Me and the boys looked at each other for a second in disbelief, "We're The Seaweed Pirates," I said.

"Niiice, I like it," he said and flipped a switch. The on air sign lit up red behind his head.

"Aloha beach goers and listeners afar. You are listening to Island Radio. I'm your host, Billy the Bird and we are flying high with special guests who just washed in from their last voyage of pillaging and plundering the fridge, haha, it's The Seaweed Pirates. They sail around and perform where they land, say hello," he said and pushed a mic towards us.

"Hey, thanks for having us on," I said. "Um I'm Joe, I sing. This is Dave, he plays guitar. This is Sean, he plays the djembe and," I was about to say something about a band mate who just left but made a quick decision not to and said, "And yeah we sail around jamming our songs shore to shore making more up as we go." I said confidently.

"Hey," the guys leaned in and said into the microphone.

"Great, well, why don't you play us some of your favorites," Billy said and I laughed because we only had those three songs really.

"Haha, ok for sure," I said and looked at the boys who looked nervous. "Like we always do bruddas," I said and counted them off.

Dave was strumming, Sean was drumming and I started singing, It was an absolute blur of perfection. By the time we finished playing people were calling in from all over wanting more.

"They love you guys!" he said.

"Well, you'll see us when we hit your shore," I said and that was it. He ended the broadcast and thanked us and his listeners for a great show and tuning in. We all thanked him and were out the door as fast as we had gone in.

"What the fuck!?" Sean asked.

"Did that really just happen?" Dave asked.

"Yep," I said but I wasn't sure either. I blacked out halfway through and don't remember it at all but it happened and it was great from what I was understanding.

"It's only 2:30, we said goodbye to Booger, we ate lunch and played on the radio?!" Dave said sounding like he was questioning reality.

"Damn, it's only 2:30," I said in disbelief myself.

"What should we do?" Dave asked.

"Go home and burn," Sean said jokingly and laughed but it actually wasn't a bad idea.

"Shit we might have to do that there's so much time before the show," I said.

"Not really. The amount of time it takes to get back to the dock and back to the boat and then chill and then try to make it back before 5 sounds impossible," Dave said.

"Really? I feel like if we stop talking and get going we'll make it," I said.

"K, let's go," Dave said sounding unsure but willing.

"Nice," Sean didn't care if we made it back or not.

"We could be on the boat by three," I said as we walked back quickly to the marina, I think we all half expected to see Booger still standing at the entrance waiting with all his stuff but he was gone and the spot was empty. I felt like we all got glum again walking by the spot, on the way to our dinghy.

"Yo, we were just on the radio!?" I said trying to break the silence with sheer excitement. It worked.

"Yeahh what?!" Dave said.

"So crazy," Sean said.

"Oh wait!" I said pointing to a convenience store across the street and we all ran over. "We gotta save at least 5 or 10 bucks for a couple more nights of gigs to make this money back, but let's get whatever," I said.

"NICE!" Sean shouted and ran in.

"Is that a good idea?" Dave asked sounding concerned.

"We can make that money back plus more. Let's celebrate. I'm grabbing some blunts, papers, soda, and candy. Ohh nah, nah, a candy ice cream bar," I said practically drooling, the ice cream part got him. It was so hot out ice cream was the obvious solution. We both ran in, the cashier looked freaked out.

"No food stamps!" he yelled at us. I flashed the cash we had left and he shut up.

We got our munchies, went to our dinghy, and headed back to our boat for a celebratory blunt session real quick and then back to perform. We were living the life.

But on the way back we saw the dready dude again, with less of a mandatory deadline I decided to finally stop and introduce ourselves properly.

He waved at us. We waved at him and I started slowing down.

"What are you doing?" Dave asked.

"Saying hi," I said and pulled up close to his boat.

"Hey," he said.

"What's up man, I'm Joe this is Sean and Dave," I pointed. "We just see you every day and were wondering if you smoke and if you want to join us right now in smoking a fat blunt?" I said.

"Sure," he said, "I'm Travis."

"Nice is this your boat?" I asked.

"Yeah," he said.

"Dude so beautiful, you wanna smoke here or on ours? You're welcome to come over," I said.

"Where's it at?" he asked and I pointed.

"Over there, the one with the green stripe and matching sail cover," I said.

"Cool, yeah. We can smoke here," he said. He was in the middle of doing something on his boat I could tell.

"Word!" I said excited to smoke with a new friend and to board this very cool ship. "We shall be right back," I yelled taking off towards our vessel.

"K," he shouted and continued doing whatever he was doing maybe fixing something I thought.

I brought us back to our ship quickly and began rolling a blunt.

"That's cool huh?" I said.

"Yeah, he seems chill," Dave said.

"Yeah," Sean said smiling. We were all happy and so we should be. We were doing some cool stuff.

"I still can't believe we were just on the radio and people from other states were calling in for us!" I said.

"Yeah like is that even real?" Dave asked and we all laughed.

"So crazy," Sean said.

"Alright good to go," I said holding up the blunt.

"Time check," Dave said.

"3:15," Sean said.

"Let's go let's go!" I shouted bolting out the cabin door and into our dinghy with the instruments still waiting, ready for tonight's performance. The boys jumped in and we were off, headed back to Travis' boat.

When we pulled up though he wasn't on the deck any longer.

"Yo," I called for him thinking he was down in his cabin or something in one of the hulls of the catamaran maybe. "Yo ho, it's me Joe," I said in a pirate voice and getting anxious. We wanted to smoke and get back to shore to secure a spot for our performance at sunset.

"Maybe he left," Dave said and just then he popped up out of the water near the shore of the island next to us.

"Aye," I yelled, "What are you doin'?"

"Fishing," he said and held up a yellow pole that looked too short to be a fishing pole.

"Haha what are you really doing?" I asked suddenly suspicious of whatever he was really doing because it didn't look like fishing to me. Looked more like he might be poking around down in the water searching for something.

He swam back over to his boat and climbed up and held out the pole. It had prongs on one end and looked like something to cook hotdogs on over an open fire.

"Y'all never heard of spear fishing?" he asked in amazement.

"Ohh, that's what that is," I said.

"Cool," Sean said.

"How do you do that?" Dave asked.

"I'll teach ya if you want," Travis offered.

"Damn that would be sick! I've been fishing a couple times but only with a fishing pole and bait and I didn't like it, but this is like some primal shit," I said excited to try but remembered we had plans. "Shoot, we actually were going to smoke this in celebration that we just got on the radio out of the blue and then we usually play for money where the cruise ships come in," I said.

"I saw the instruments. I was wondering," Travis said.

"Yeah let's spark it," Sean said and I handed it to him.

"Fire it up," I said. "Oh do you care if we burn right here or you wanna go down into the hull?" I asked.

"Here's good," he said smiling and Sean started smoking the blunt. "You sure you don't wanna try real quick?" Travis asked me. He could tell I really did want to.

"Ahh I don't think I'll have time but fuck it," I said.

"Sweet you guys interrupted me catching some dinner," he said smiling and handed me a spear, goggles and a pair of flippers for my feet.

Sean and Dave were happy to be smoking the blunt with two less people and enjoying all the space of Travis' boat. The whole thing was basically a large deck with a tiki hut on top and a sail so you could walk around freely like a patio on the sea.

"We really need these flippers?" I asked laughing.

"Oh yah man, they make you fast enough to catch up to the fish," he said seriously but with kindness. He was a mystical dude.

"Ok word," I said nodding as we sat down on the edge of his boat and put the flipper fins on our feet.

"Ok when we get in there be very still and ready to hold your breath a long time," he said. I continued to nod. "When you get down there man, you're going to notice if you relax and be one with the ocean-life, that the fish are staring right at you in astonishment, like they know you're a higher being. I know you feel bad about the killing part and so do I, but you have to look at it like that too, and you are about to bring them to the next life. We do what needs to be done to survive. Find the right one like a grouper or a hog fish, something big and start chasing it," he said. I hung on every word.

"You want this?" Sean asked over to me while him and Dave continued smoking. I did want it but I wanted to learn this skill, too.

"Just smoke it, I'll roll another later," I said interrupting Travis.

"Sorry go on bro, so how do I actually spear one?" I asked.

"Oh yeah, take this bungy cord put it around your arm," he said demonstrating with his spear. The spears were fiberglass like a ski pole or something and had prongs at one end and a bungy cord loop on the other end. I had thought that was just so he didn't lose it but it had a purpose. It was actually a mechanism of some type. He went on explaining.

"With the sling around your arm you try to stretch it and grab as far up the rod as you can with the same hand that's looped, then when you're ready to fire, let go," he said and did what he was saying and stretched it, reached up, grabbed the middle of the rod and let go which sent the spear flying forward, shooting out of his hand, but he caught it before it flew away. "Like that," he said smiling.

"Duude nice!" I said.

"Ready?" he asked about to jump in.

"Wait any tips or tricks on how to really get one," I said.

"When you're chasing one down and you start to gain on him, the fish knows it's the end for him and in a last ditch effort stops and turns to the side to appear larger and scare off his approaching enemy and that is the moment," Travis said.

"Whoah," I said. "Heavy," shocked at this in-depth visualization he gave me.

"Haha," he laughed and we hopped in the warm water.

"Won't be hard to see them down there," I said looking into the water laughing.

"Yeah, it's gorgeous. Would you like to follow me around and see how I do it first?" Travis asked.

"Yeah man let's go!" I said anxiously.

"Cool follow me," and he took a huge breath and plunged down into the light blue water.

I did the same and followed diving down, it was only about 14 feet deep but there was lots of reef and seaweed for all types of fish to be hiding in. We went straight to the bottom and swam among the colorful fish. I followed him weaving through tall strands of seaweed I had previously had the bad experience with, but I felt safe with Travis and always had my knife since then. I felt like a big fish as we used mostly our legs flippering along the ocean floor steadily. It was amazing how much faster these things made me swim. I was running out of breath when we came upon a very large cave-like thing in the ground. I got freaked out and started swimming in reverse and then up to the surface for air waiting for Travis to come up, but he didn't.

I didn't want to lose him but I didn't really want to go in the cave and it looked like that's exactly where he went. I gulped a mass of air and went under again quickly swimming for the mouth of the cave thing to find him. As I swam up to it, I realized it was man made, maybe a metal or wood structure but definitely not a natural cave. It had just been grown over by seaweed and covered in sand. The fish had taken over and Mother Nature had reclaimed it for her own. With no sign of Travis I started to swim in slowly ready for anything spear in hand. I could barely see. It might not have been a real cave but it felt like one.

Out of the corner of my eye a large shadowy figure was hurdling towards me fast. I held the spear with both hands and turned to face it quickly. It was just Travis coming out for air. I followed him up to get some myself and see what the plan was.

"Damn dude I thought you were a shark or something," I said laughing when we breached the surface.

"I thought you were going to spear me," he said laughing back.

"Na," I said still laughing. The sun was getting lower in the sky and I could see the boys were smoking still but it was turning into a roach.

"I don't want to leave them waiting too long," I said.

"Yeah, there was nothing down there," he said.

"No worries you still taught me a lot man. It was fun, thank you," I said thinking he was done, too.

"Ah, you are welcome for sure man. If you're leaving just put that stuff on the deck but I still gotta catch dinner," he said. We both paused while I thought for a second. I saw Sean and Dave still puffing the roach. "We have to swim back to the boat still, I'm going to get one on the way," he said smiling with the setting sun behind him just a silhouette of dreads and a man savagely holding his spear. It was getting darker above the water and below.

"True!" I said, "Right behind ya," and we dove back down dodging the seaweed sea monsters I was creating in my mind as we hugged the ocean floor trying to blend in with fish.

He started swimming left then right, kicking up sand, clouding the already darkened water. I was losing him in the action as he turned into a blur disappearing in the distance. I slowed down and went up for air but I didn't see him. I went right back down to see the sand had settled and Travis kneeling on the ocean floor over whatever his spear was pinning to the ground. He pulled out a knife from his leg holster and stabbed again for the kill shot to make sure it wasn't suffering, but then he put his head down in a praying position for a moment then brought it up.

"Who wants dinner!" Travis said proudly bursting out of the water with his fish on a stick.

"NO WAY," I shouted. "That was epic man," I yelled swimming over to him and pulled the goggles off my face.

"What? You didn't think I could do it?" Travis asked.

"Nah, I've just never seen it done man. Good job!" I said. "What was that little thing you did at the end after you stabbed it with your knife?" I asked him.

"Oh I just say a little thing after the kill, thanking them for their sacrifice and saying sorry I had to do it to survive and I wish them well in the afterlife," he said quite profoundly I thought.

I was pretty speechless about the whole thing. I just nodded to let him know I understood, but I was amazed in the spirituality of the way this dude got dinner. It was like a religious experience for him to have a meal but maybe that's the way it should be, I thought realizing so many people would never get that feeling from a drive-thru. Maybe we were taking it for granted the way we get food.

"Right, let's get her to the boat before sharks come," he said nonchalantly and swam to his ship holding the spear up while he swam with the fish in the air. I guess trying not to get blood in the water.

"Sharks huh?" I said as we reached the boat and climbed up on deck. "Are they bad out here?" I asked but Sean and Dave walked over excited to hear what happened and see what we got.

"Whoah nice!" Sean said seeing the fish on the spear. It was a good size, too. Travis held it up smiling.

"I was going to ask how it went but looks like it went well," Dave said and laughed a little checking out the fish as well.

"I almost speared Travi-boy here," I said laughing. "Thought he was a shark," I added slapping Travis on the back. He laughed.

"What? Really! How?" Dave asked excited.

Sean looked at us not sure whether to laugh or not but definitely shocked.

"Na, it was fine," Travis said. "Hey I'm gonna cook this up for us," he said and went down into one of the catamaran hulls.

"Oooh nihice," I said to Travis then started telling the boys the story of how I almost speared Travis, but Dave interrupted me.

"Hey we missed the 5 o'clock thing," he said looking concerned.

"Oh fuck, I completely forgot, I thought we really needed this skill for low money times, well we can still play the burger dog spot," I said.

"Yeah, true," Dave said.

"Worrd," Sean said and Travis came back up with the fish wrapped in a bunch of tinfoil in one hand and a little grill like ours in the other.

The sun set down and we all sat around the little grill our faces lit by the flickering flames.

"Y'all wanna play me some of your music?" Travis asked. "I'd love to hear it while we wait for this to cook," he added.

"Yeah man!" I said. "Let's play him a jam," and I jumped up and grabbed the instruments from our dinghy tied up still to Travis' ship waiting to take us to work. I handed the drum to Sean and the guitar to Dave still sitting on the deck, "Bobbin' boys," I said and stayed standing, we played the song in our element actually bobbing on the boat and Travis felt it.

"That's my new favorite song in the world," he said dead serious. "Can you play it again?" he asked.

"Haha, it's one of my favorites, too, brudda. Yeah definitely," I said. "Glad you like it," I added and turned back to the boys.

"You good?" making sure they were down.

"Yaha!" Sean said.

"Absolutely," Dave said and I smiled counting them off.

"2, 3, We're bobbin on the ocean," we played it again and we were all just thoroughly living in the moment, enjoying each other's company and this unique experience. We ended and it was perfect timing.

"Fish is ready," Travis said while applauding our little performance.

"Nice, I'm stoked to try if you don't mind," I said as he unfolded the tinfoil and revealed the fish, the whole fish, scales, eyes, fins and all.

"Oh damn," Sean said and I laughed.

It was beautifully golden and cooked looking but disgustingly whole still, like it swam through a fire and died.

"Um I'm actually all set on that but I appreciate it all the same," Dave said standing up and looking at it more closely then backing away.

"Sure?" Travis asked picking off a piece and eating it. "It's delicious," he said with his mouth full.

"I'll try some," I said eagerly stepping up to the plate.

"Here try an eye," Travis said. "They're great calcium."

"Haha shut the fuck up," I said laughing.

"No I'm serious man it's good," he said.

"Ewww haha," Sean laughed. "Fuck no."

"Blah," Dave made a puke noise.

"You first," I said and he plucked out the eye and tossed it in his mouth.

"Let me see," I said in disbelief.

He stuck out his tongue. "LAHH!" he said sticking out his tongue and then pulled it back in closed his mouth and chewed making an eccentric face.

"Damn alright if you say so," and I plucked out the other, looked at it eye to eye for a second and tossed it into my mouth quickly chewing. "Aw shit it's not bad, little chalky," I said.

"Yeahh ya see, there you go bro," Travis said and we fist bumped in the orange-yellow flickers of the grill light in the night.

"Thanks for everything dude. It's cool meeting someone cool out here. We should do this every night!" I said excitedly.

"Yeah this is awesome," Dave said.

"I'm down but we gotta cook it a different way next time," Sean said.

"Great meeting you guys, too," Travis said, "But I'm actually leaving tomorrow."

"You're joking man! Are you serious?" I said but looking at him I could tell he was, "Damn dude that sucks."

"Yeah we shoulda stopped by sooner," Dave said.

"Lame," Sean said.

"It really doesn't suck though, I'm going to see my dad who's up anchored at a better island, but I am going to be thinking about you guys and I'll definitely have your song stuck in my head. Y'all should come with me," Travis said.

"Oh your dad? That's cool. He lives on a boat, too! Damn, I don't know man, we just started getting settled in here, figuring things out, making money, haha. I'm glad you like our song man. We're gonna miss you and we've only chilled for a few hours, heck thanks again for everything," I said and pulled him in for a one-armed hug.

"Nice meeting you, Travis, thanks for teaching Joey to spear. He'll probably end up trying to teach us, haha," Dave said laughing.

"I'll spear some," Sean said laughing, too.

"We'll have to buy one soon or make one, alright, well, we better get rocking man, gotta make that paper tonight," I said enthusiastically.

"Why do you guys need money?" Travis asked.

"Umm," Dave said.

"You know gas, grass, food, whatever," I said.

"I can get you gas and I showed you how to get food plus there's a free dinghy dock and a pool and an anchorage there," Travis said.

"And we still got plenty of ganja if we slow it down," Dave said.

"You for real? You can get us gas?" I asked Travis considering it for a second.

"Yeah I know a guy," he said and I didn't question it.

"Ah man, I hope we meet again," I said and gave another one-armed hug.

"Me too man, you guys are cool, here have this," he said handing me the yellow spear he let me borrow earlier.

"What! No way! I can't man," I said.

"I gotta few bro. I want you to have it," he said pushing it into my hands.

"Nice!" Sean shouted.

"Alright if you insist," I said smiling and taking the spear. "Dude you're the fucking best, thank you so much. We're gonna hit you up if or when we ever get moving again," I said.

He and Dave had exchanged numbers at some point earlier. I didn't pay it much attention because I didn't have a phone, but now it seemed like it might come in handy down the road or river wherever it may be.

We said goodbye and went to shore ready to hit the streets and perform. I did really wish we had met Travis sooner, but everything happens for a reason and who knows maybe we wouldn't have been on the radio if we were just chilling spear fishing all day, but it was great to finally meet him and make a new friend who was doing what we were doing kind of, and who knows, "maybe we will link up eventually," I thought as we walked up to the burger dog stand to jam.

Along the way we saw the usual belligerent debauchery but juxtaposed to the day we had on the water it all seemed so different.

"Rhonda!" I said.

"My boys, heard you on the radio earlier, great job!" she said with her arms outstretched towards us with burger dogs.

The streets were lit up bright with street lights and lights from every bar plus the little lights of the dog stand.

"Ya heard us?!" I said laughing and amazed.

"Yeah everyone listens to Island Radio, man," Rhonda said.

"The Seaweed Pirates are famous boys," I said laughing.

"Haha," Dave and Sean laughed scarfing down their burger dogs. I joined them stuffing a burger dog into my face and set up our spot at the tree across from the dog stand. Dave pulled out the guitar and I propped open the case so people could see our name clearly.

"Hey, what happened to the other guy? Little Booger?" Rhonda asked noticing he was gone, too.

"He left," I said.

"Left the band or the island?" Rhonda asked.

"Maybe both I guess, I don't know," I said trying to brush it off.

"Awe, poor Booger brains," she said and continued cooking dogs.

"Yeah he'll be alright," I said and looked at the boys. "Ready?" I asked them as they got into position.

"Ready!" Dave said holding the guitar.

"Yup," Sean said and we started rocking and the people started flocking.

The night started off right as the drunken tourists lined up for their grub and tossed us dollars shouting our name, "The Seaweed Pirates!"

At one point in the night some people came up to us and I could tell they were a little different than the tourists around us. They didn't really fit in. It looked more like they might own the place or some hotels or something. It was two old gentlemen and an older lady looking like rich oil tycoons out for a night on the town. The obvious leader stopped right in front of us, ignoring our pretend stage space and asked, "What's your favorite song you wrote, son?" looking me right in the eyes, almost uncomfortably, but I had a good feeling.

"The Sunset Song," I said confidently.

"Alright play it for me," the man said and dropped a twenty dollar bill in the case fresh and crispy.

"Hit it boys," I said smiling and we killed it. The man didn't step back an inch. He didn't blink, smile, or flinch, he just said, "You should be hitting a drum, too," and tossed another twenty dollars in.

"Who are you?" Dave asked shocked.

The man smiled and winked.

"Keep it up, I really liked that," he said turning away and the three of them were gone in the crowd of people.

"What the fuck!" Sean said holding up the two twenty dollar bills. I stood there shocked, pretty sure I knew exactly who that was and I couldn't believe it.

"That was Jimmy fucking Buffet," I said still paralyzed.

"No way! Was it really?" Dave said starting to freak out.

"I think so," I said.

"But you're not sure," Dave said.

"I mean it looked like him, sounded like him, and he gave us more money than anyone the entire time we've been here soo.." I said.

"I don't know," Dave said skeptically.

"Who's Jimmy Buffet?" Sean asked.

"Who's Jimmy Buffet!" I repeated. "Who's Jimmy Buffet? Come on man," and I started to sing Cheeseburger in Paradise.

"Oh oh oh yeah, I love that song," Sean said and then it hit him too. "Oh no way, that's wild. Was it really?"

"Think so man, I'm gonna say yeah it was and that's my story and I'm sticking to it," I said.

"Hey, you guys gonna play or what?" Rhonda asked.

"Jimmy Buffet was just here!" I yelled at her excitedly.

"He's always here," she said. "Now can you get back to work and bring me more customers please. I got more dogs for ya," she said holding up more burger dogs.

She was great and I was thankful but it had been a long crazy day, "Ah, I'm beat but thank you so much. We'll see you tomorrow for sure," I said and looked at the guys who started packing up.

"Okay, then see ya tomorrow," Rhonda said quickly getting back to work.

Sean and Dave grabbed the gear and we walked down the main street heading home for the night finally. Exhausted, we walked silently as usual, each recapping in his own mind the day we just had while silently observing our surroundings of lights and fights.

"Yo that's that Jimmy guy! I think," Dave said.

"Jimmy Buffet!" Sean said anxiously probably thinking about cheeseburgers again.

"Where? Which Jimmy?" I asked trying to see what he was talking about.

He pointed, "There fighting! That kid with the stool," he said.

There was Mr. Jimmy in an all-out brawl throwing a dude into a wall and then being thrown himself into the wall. The dude smashed Mr. Jimmy's face off a pole that was holding the deck above them up. Blood squirted from his face and they started exchanging blows. We ran over to break it up but the people around them had already stopped it.

"Damn, Mr. Jimmy, you alright bro!?" I said.

"Feeling great!" he said wiping blood from his face and flicking it onto the ground.

"What was that all about?" Dave asked, I wasn't gonna.

"That asshole stole my wife," Mr. Jimmy said without looking at us and continued to walk.

"You have a wife?" Sean asked and laughed. He just seemed too young. He was like our age, maybe a little older. Then he pointed her out back in the crowd. She was with some other man and the guy who Mr. Jimmy had just fought.

"Yes, I was a happily married man and now I'm sad. I paid $50 bucks for her," he said almost crying.

"Uh man hate to break it to ya but she was a," Dave started to say something but I cut him off.

"I'm sure she was a great lady man, but you'll find someone better someday," I said and gave Dave a look like let's just leave it alone and go. He understood.

"Take it easy, Mr. Jimmy man, see ya around," I said and pulled Sean and Dave the other direction.

"Peace out," Dave said.

"Peace," Sean said.

But Mr. Jimmy kept walking with his head down and didn't really acknowledge us.

"What is up with that dude?" Sean whispered as we got some distance between us.

"I don't know man, I kinda feel bad for him," I said.

"Yeah, me too," Dave said and we continued home to the dinghy dock.

We got in our little lifeboat and cruised home to our sailboat in the sea, with the breeze blowing through our hair giving us a Ben Franklin air-bath, as we continued replaying the day from start to end. It was that autopilot feel, we arrived at our vessel before I even knew it, daydreaming all the way.

We pulled up, tied off and I took a deep loud breath in and let it out.

"I feel ya," Sean said climbing into the boat.

"Dudes what a fucking day," I said.

"Yep, I'm going right to sleep," Dave said unlocking the cabin doors.

"Same," Sean said.

"I'm gonna take a couple puffs out here," I said in an almost melancholy kind of way.

"K," they said and went in to sleep.

I grabbed my guitar pipe and sat on the bow with it smoking and looking out at the islands and boats all lit up and I thought about life and the grand scheme of things. We were on a journey which led to a treasure hunt which led to creating a name for ourselves and possibly a career in music we hadn't even planned on, but the career part freaked me out and thinking back to Rhonda asking us to get back to "work". We weren't here to work, we were here for adventure, and to get away from people and drama of the mainland, were we really doing that any more, I wondered. Did we want to stay and make money and party and make a name for ourselves, or continue the adventure and live for free off the sea, maybe find Sensemilla Island? Staying sounded great in theory, but that's not what we wanted and I knew it. We weren't trying to perform every night. We wanted to chill and enjoy the ride, but it was starting to be a job. We weren't on vacation anymore, we were entertaining vacationers. It was fun at first, but sitting there, smoking in the night under the moon light and smelling that salty breeze, I knew we were ready to move on.

I suddenly remembered that Travis was leaving in the morning and he invited us to join him. If he was serious that would be perfect I thought, cause he could just lead the way. It would be fun. I took some more rips and held them in deep, trying to smoke away my new anxiousness. I needed to get to sleep if we wanted to depart in the morning. I wrote a quick little sea shanty that went like this:

>We're sailing to Sensemilla Island,
>We're smoking weed and drinking on the way,
>Away to another land we are sailing,
>We're drinking rum and smoking all the way.
>The time has come to pull up on the anchor,
>We'll hoist the sails, set them, then we're free!
>The wind is at our backs, the sun is setting,
>And soon there'll be a pirate-looting spree.

I quickly went into the cabin smiling to myself and found the nearest empty bench and passed out anxious to tell them the new plan and hoped they'd be down.

DAY 19

The first sign of light I sprung off the bench wide awake like I hadn't even slept.

"Dudes, dudes," I shouted trying to wake them up quickly, "Dudes wake up!" I said.

"What's up? What's wrong?" Dave sat up from the V-hull thinking something was wrong and looking concerned.

"New plan!" I shouted. "Let's follow Travis and keep exploring," I shouted.

"OK," Sean yelled sitting up like he had been listening but didn't want to move until now.

"Really? Why the sudden change?" Dave said.

"'Cause we're not here to work. We're on an adventure," I said.

"Ok, I'm down," Dave said and we started jumping around with excitement cheering for our new journey.

"What time's he leaving? Did he say?" Dave asked.

"Oh, shit, true I don't know," I said, "Text him."

"K," Dave said but he didn't answer.

I ran out onto the deck and stood on top of the cabin looking out to make sure he was still there and sure enough he was sailing away, slowly leaving the anchorage.

"Let's go! Come with me, Sean!" I yelled and we hopped into the dinghy.

"What are you doing?" Dave asked shouting as we pulled away.

"I'm gonna ask Travis to wait for us!" I yelled and sped off towards Travis who was still cruising away. I completely disregarded the unwritten no-wake rule around other boats probably full of sleepy sailors as we went top speed bouncing through the little ripples of the morning waters between boats 'til we caught up to Travis who was just really about to hit the open waters.

"Wait! Travis! Wait bro!" I yelled pulling up alongside him.

He had the sails up but there was no wind and he was just motoring slowly. He put it in neutral and so did we. Sean grabbed onto Travis' boat.

"Hey guys, I wanted to say bye but I didn't want to wake you. Glad you cruised over!" Travis said joyfully.

"Bro, we changed our minds, we wanna come with you!" I said.

"Yeah," Sean yelled holding our boats together.

"Wow awesome! What made you change your minds?" he asked.

"We want more adventure," I said smiling and sat back into the dinghy ready to steer us back to get our boat.

"The more the merrier," Travis threw up his arms, and said, "I'll be waiting here for you guys."

"K, we just gotta switch this engine over and pull anchor, shouldn't take too long," I said and cruised off quickly.

"Woohoo!" Sean shouted as I whipped through the boats.

"HEY you damn kids!" some angry man yelled from his boat bow. I didn't even look. We'd be gone soon enough and we'd never see him again I thought to myself as we pulled up and Sean tied us off.

"Don't leave, hold on," I said to Sean, "I'm going to switch this over now," pointing to the engine.

"I'll keep ya steady," Sean said holding onto the sides of our ship and standing in the dinghy.

"Everything good?" Dave came running over to us at the back of the boat, still in a dinghy standing.

"Yup, he's waiting for us, grab me the bungies," I said with haste.

He retrieved them for me quickly and we secured the engine in case I dropped it, it would still have a lifeline.

"Nice," I said, "Thank you," and I heaved the heavy engine up and into place.

Click snap the engine was locked in.

"Anchor!" I yelled and Sean ran up with Dave and pulled it up.

"It's stuck!" Sean yelled.

"Pull harder, we gotta go, he's waiting!" I yelled.

They continued trying as hard as they could.

"Oh fuck," I yelled. "Stop," and I dove into the water.

The carabiner clip I had put down there must have worked so well it was still holding us captive. I found it and undid the clip quickly, swimming to the surface.

"My bad, I forgot about that clip!" I said laughing and swimming back to the boat then climbed up the ladder. "K, boys, hoist her up," I said in my pirate voice and we started the engine.

"All good," Sean yelled pulling the anchor up onto the bow and securing it to the bowsprit.

"Hang on," I yelled and we started moving, this time I had to take it a little slower. It was different than the dinghy and I felt a little rusty. The last thing we wanted was to hit a boat before we left. I successfully maneuvered us through the minefield of live-aboard boats around us and stopped right next to Travis.

"Ahoy matey," I yelled.

"Hey, you guys made it. I was beginning to think you changed your minds again," Travis said laughing, hanging off the side of his ship, leaning out for a high-five from Sean, who was leaning out as well to grab on to his ship before we collided.

"Haha yeah long story but we're ready!" I said.

"Awesome. Let me just pull up anchor, I wasn't sure how long it was going to take you," Travis said still laughing.

"Haha alright, we'll pull up over here then follow you," I said pointing ahead.

"Cool," he said.

"Push us away," I said to Sean, so we didn't bump his beautifully handcrafted hand-rails along the side of his ship.

"K," Sean said pushing us away and I motored forward and then into neutral, bobbing, waiting for Travis.

"Oh yeah, the sails," I said thinking out loud.

"Haha," Dave and Sean laughed.

"Haha alright, you guys do your thing with the front sail, I'll get the main sail," I said leaving the engine running in neutral and climbed up to the mast to uncover and hoist the main sail. "Hey, grab the big green one for the shit wind days!" I yelled as they went down to get the sail.

"Got it," Dave said.

They both started clipping it to the line and preparing it while I finished hoisting the main sail up.

"Woo alright not bad," I said out of breath and seeing they were just finishing, too.

"Little slower without Booger, but we still got it boys!" I shouted.

"Yeww!" Sean yelled and hopped back to the helm with me.

"You smell something burning?!" I said quickly getting the crew on its toes.

"No?" Dave said, freaked out, sniffing the air rampantly.

"Me either" I said laughing "Let's get smoking."

"Haha," Sean laughed, "Yes."

"Oh man haha alright, I'll roll us a doober," Dave said.

"Perfect," I said winking and using my pirate voice. It felt good to be back on the sea, smoking the weeds, and living like pirate outlaws.

SSWEEOUTTT! A loud whistle noise came up behind us and we looked as Travis cruised past us, sailing his ship, gliding across the glistening, tropical waters like magic, carried by the lightest wind.

"Yo ho," we all yelled and I floored the engine, gassing it to catch up.

"Set the sails, boys, hold on tight!" I yelled forgetting to warn them as they lurched back and we gunned it forward.

"Shihit," Dave yelled out.

"Wooo," Sean shouted then they regained their legs and angled the sails to catch wind as I steered us in the right direction.

"All set, that's all we got, Captain!" Dave yelled.

"K, get back here and scroll us up that doober, ya boob," I shouted then slowed the engine down to see how much of our movement was from the wind.

We slowed down considerably, but it wasn't a race. We were off though, leaving that strange but wonderful place behind in our wake.

It might have been the most gorgeous day yet, the sun was up and there wasn't a cloud in the sky except the ones we were making smoking the joint Dave just rolled up for us all, as we gently cruised through real life oasis.

Travis slowed down by letting his massive sail out a little, releasing some wind and allowing us to catch up for a moment.

"EYE MATE HOW YE BE!" I yelled pulling up alongside his vessel.

"Wish the winds were faster but perfect weather all the same," Travis said using a pirate voice and laughing and we all laughed.

"Want a hit?" I yelled across to Travis in his boat. We were parallel helms lined up. He was practically right beside me already.

"Sure!" he yelled laughing and tied his steering wheel steady with a rope, like an autopilot.

"Haha okay," I yelled with the joint in my mouth. I steered closer trying to get us close enough to pass it.

"Little closer," Travis yelled. Sean and Dave watched on as we attempted the stunt nervously.

"Alright," I said inching closer, as I leaned out towards him reaching with the joint and I saw Sean reaching for his boat but it was too late.

Crunch! We hit a wave and connected boats bashing into each other in mid air and came down with the horrible sound of wood breaking.

"Fuuck!" I yelled.

"No biggie," Travis yelled back puffing on the doobie and grabbing his wheel after the sort of successful pass off.

"You sure, dude, I'm so sorry," I said looking at the damage.

"Damn," Dave said.

"Ouch," Sean said.

"Yeah, no, it's all good brother. I made these by hand, I can make more," Travis shouted, ripping the doobie.

I didn't even want to ask for it back after that but he cruised over to us again and ran up and passed it to Sean while we were close for a second then continued sailing. We were killing it. The trip was starting off pretty great and I felt like we had made the right choice leaving. Out of nowhere we were surrounded by dolphins jumping and flipping in the air, staying with us like they knew us. For hours they swam beside us to the point where we were naming them. We smoked and sailed slowly but surely, traversing the sea and being free, just a leisurely cruise, but I noticed Travis was way ahead of us. Travis must have noticed, too, because at that same moment he texted Dave.

Dave showed me the text while I steered.

Travis: [You guys want me to wait for y'all?]

I read it and thought for a second. I did want him to wait but I didn't want to slow him down.

Dave: [Na man don't let us slow you down. We'll be right behind you.]

Travis: [Ok cool thanks its straight ahead another 40 miles or so.]

Dave: [k text us when you get there!]

And that was it. We were alone with the dolphins as we passed island after island and eventually they even left us when the sun went down.

"Well boys who's the least tired?" I asked. We had made one dire error. We forgot to plan out who would sail through the night and who would nap and even then someone would have to pull a double with us being down a man.

"I'm good," Sean said.

"Oh thank God, I'm so ready to lay down," Dave said.

"Alright brother, we got this," I said and we started going faster out of nowhere. "Whoah, would ya look at that, a boost!" I yelled as the wind picked up suddenly.

"Nice, you know where I'll be if you need me," Dave said sounding tired and I couldn't really see his face that well, it was so dark already.

"EYE MATE!" I yelled.

"EYE!" Sean yelled and laughed as the winds continued to increase and we were going 7 mph it read on the light-up GPS glowing in the darkness.

"Holy shit, dude!" I yelled. "That's the fastest yet."

A bolt of lightning cracked through the sky and thundered all around us.

"Fuuhuck," Sean said laughing again.

"Turn on the radio mate," I hollered to Sean who ran and got the hand-held and switched it on.

"Winds of 15-20 miles an hour rushing from the Southeast. Put life jackets on and head for nearest coast. Winds of," a robotic male voice repetitively blasted.

"We're alright. Shut it off," I said and we continued hauling ass through the now choppy waters and pitch black sky.

No moon, no stars, only the occasional lightning strike which started getting closer as it began to rain.

"Alright, put it back on mate," I yelled in a pirate voice.

Sean put it back on sitting listening with me on the high side by the helm.

"Put life jackets on and head for nearest coast."

"Haha!" I laughed loudly in a sarcastic way. "We don't need no stinking life jackets," I yelled.

Bang! Thunder boomed as lightning crashed right over our heads now more frequently. The rain drops catching the blue white light by the thousands over my head like we were sailing through the stratosphere.

"Winds of 35-40 miles an hour rushing from the Southeast," the voice continued to repeat itself with only the numbers of the speed changing as the approaching squall increased and we could feel it correlating with the robot man on the two-way radio.

"Oh shit! That's fucking crazy!" I yelled over the storm at Sean as we began to heel over further. A loud thud came from inside the cabin. Dave must have rolled off a bench.

"What the fuck?" Dave screamed trying to stand propping himself in the doorway of the cabin.

"SQUALL!" I yelled.

"Winds of 70 mph," the voice said from the radio.

"Get the life jackets," I yelled, but the wind took us over. "Untie the!" I shouted into the blackness but I couldn't see if anyone was doing anything. I jumped up from the helm, "Hold this steady!" I said to Sean, grabbing him by the shoulder as the boat was being pushed over. The lightning flash revealed the fear in his eyes and Dave reaching out with the life jackets.

The ship was on its side and taking on water fast. In the flashes of light I saw Dave hang on for dear life, trying to hand out life jackets. Sean frozen in time and space but steady on the wheel. I let out the main sail and dove to the other side for the front sail line so I could let it out, but it was under water. I reached up to the mast which was now parallel with the water and right over my head to un-cleat the line from the mast which would lose it, lose it, but it had to be done or we were done. The massive sail was catching all of the squall in it bringing us down to Davey Jones' locker. I let it out probably at the last possible moment before we could take on anymore water and looked back to see Sean still sitting like a statue at the helm in the flashes of light and ran back to him as the boat bounced back to its proper position now that it wasn't being forced over by wind. I made a huge mistake of leaving that big green sail on. That's exactly why it was only for light winds.

"Everyone alright?" I yelled, trying to get a head count as it seemed the storm had passed as quickly as it came through, the definition of a squall.

"EYE," Sean yelled coming back to life.

"Dave where are ya mate?" I yelled. "Dave!" and I got back on the helm and fired up the engine. "Find Dave," I said to Sean. The storm started to die down but the rain never let up. "I'm gonna get us out of this, gassing it and speeding towards whatever land we could find."

"Alright," Sean shouted and went down into the cabin to check on Dave.

I noticed we lost our front sail and the dinghy was gone, but off to my right the silhouette of an island in the distance somehow appeared there like a large black ominous object in the ocean. I was thankful to be able to make it out against the complete darkness of the night now that the lightning had stopped.

"He's good," Sean yelled.

"Alright, I see an island," I said starting to turn the ship towards it. "I'm goin' for it," I yelled and throttled through the waves, bouncing us hard as we careened towards the massive black silhouette of what I hoped to be an island.

And then crunch! A horrible grinding, smashing sound as we came to a complete stop, running aground on the unknown land. I didn't know how to feel. I was happy we were safe and out of the water, but that did not sound good to me.

"Ssshit," Sean said, putting the cabin lights on.

"Dude what the hell, man?!" I heard Dave it sounded like from the bathroom.

"Yeah, well we're safe I guess," I said sitting down as it continued to rain on my head.

"Is the boat okay?" Dave asked coming out of the bathroom.

"Haha you fuck," I said laughing. "I don't know, I'm just glad we're not out there anymore," I said not thinking they fully understood we almost just died or at least capsized, but out in the middle of nowhere, with no dinghy, and no life jackets, in shark infested waters, at night."

"Yeah," Sean said, agreeing with me and sitting down swigged a bottle of some rum.

"Gimme that," I said laughing as we sat in darkness parked on the shore of some unknown island, I took a swig and handed it back. "Welp, fuck dudes, think I'm gonna get some shut eye," I said getting up from the wheel.

"Really? We're just gonna stay here man?" Dave asked.

I hadn't planned any further. "I can't even think right now," I said.

"Isn't the boat fucked if we sit here?" Dave asked.

"Bro, I think it's fucked already," I said glumly knowing the trip was really over.

"Na man, let's get this thing outta here," he said trying to take charge.

"You gonna get down in the water and push it off this coral reef or rock or barnacled whatever we're on?" I asked hoping he'd say no.

"Yeah, I will," he said.

"Me, too," Sean said and I suddenly didn't want to be the one giving up. I was just pretty sure it was done.

"Alright bruddas, let's do this," I said and let out a big sigh.

It was still pitch black and the boat was on something and surrounded by knee-high water as we climbed down into it and walked around to the front. I could feel it was exactly what I thought it was as it poked my feet, barnacled stone and shells.

"Alright, 3, 2, push!" I yelled and the three of us shoved as hard as we could trying to get our ship to move, but it was a lot heavier than we anticipated. I started bouncing it with my shoulder and Sean did the same, "3, 2, puuush!" I yelled as we wiggled the ship slowly starting to budge it back into the sea. I could feel at the same time, sharp slices in my feet, stinging as we pushed with all our might.

"It's moving," Dave yelled.

"Get in!" I yelled as the rain still poured down on us.

I was worried this wasn't the right move to go back out into the storm, but that's what they wanted. Me and Sean continued to push until we were waist deep then climbed in and I quickly started the engine up.

"Wait!" Dave screamed again.

"There's no waiting mate!" I yelled and started heading away from the island quickly avoiding anymore reefs.

"We're taking on water!" Dave yelled.

My heart stopped along with time it felt like as frustration began to boil inside me and I could no longer hear anything. I knew what I needed to do. I whipped the boat around while I still could and throttled her straight for the island again. And this time I didn't let off.

SMASH. BOP. BOOM. THUD. CRASH. Was really the last sounds I heard as I ran aground on the island once more.

DAY 20

"Wait, wait. Don't wake him up!" I heard Dave whispering as I started to regain consciousness and I could see the light of a new day through my eye-lids.

SMACK. I slapped myself in the face because something was tickling me and it smelt like heaven or weed. I opened my eyes, it was Dave tickling my nose with a giant bud of cannabis ripe for the harvest but still on the stem.

"Am I dead?" I asked, starting to trip out, genuinely unsure, based on my last memories and that I was currently staring at Dave and the giant bud and Sean smiling in the sunlight.

"Yup and you went to heaven," Sean said, smacking me with a giant package of what appeared to be sealed and full of weed.

"AHHHH!" We all started screaming, shouting and jumping around. "Sensemilla Island!" I looked around and couldn't see weed but could smell the dankest most delicious, fruity, funky, stinky buds permeating my nostrils.

I jumped off the boat and onto the sand.

"We did it guys! We fucking did it!" I yelled running into to explore our new home.

"You did it brudda!" Sean yelled holding up the square grouper.

"Na, we did it," I said, disappearing into the jungle.

"I followed their footsteps which followed the smell. I didn't have to go too far in before I saw every flavor washed up on shore here. There were trees in trees. Pounds of weed had lodged themselves into strange hollows of trees on the island, when the tide would get high it must have washed the weed in further. The more I walked, the more weed I saw. It was absolute paradise and it was ours.

Palm trees and pot plants as far as I could see, giant bushes of fully budding herb in every direction. Purple buds, red hairy buds, frosty light blue with fluorescent pink hairs and the packages of herb ready to smoke sticking out of tree holes. I didn't care if I was dead. This was the life that I wanted. I walked up to a huge ganja plant with all its buds and went under it to see its roots. It was growing straight out of the knot hole in another tree.

"WHOAHH," I said to myself, feeling it with my hand. It had a monster stock that became one with the palm tree. I crawled out from under the weed tree and reached for a plastic and duct tape wrapped package. I ripped open the weathered wrapping and out fell a pound bag of Blue Bavarian Cream Cake OG. It had a nice label and looked legit. I opened it to sniff the glorious aroma of a bakery making fresh blueberry muffins covered in cream cheese frosting. "Haah," I breathed in and then looked at it, white with trichome crystals. It was like a winter's day in that bag of frosty goodness. I ran back to the boys with a fresh catch of square grouper of my own.

There was a cloud around our busted boat as Sean and Dave smoked it out. They sat on the side of the boat smoking and waving as I came running.

"Did you find some?" Sean said laughing.

"We thought that was the last time we'd ever see you," Dave shouted.

"Found a good one mates," I yelled smiling and climbed up on our boat and started packing a pipe.

"What are we gonna do, bro?" Dave said.

I stopped packing the pipe and looked at him, "Can I just smoke this first, please?" I asked.

"Try this one," Sean said, handing me a doobie. "Kushberry," he said raising his eyebrows and smiling.

"Mmm," I said puffing it and doing that thing fancy people do when they sip fine wine.

"Here try this one, bro," Dave said smiling now too, forgetting what he was saying he was so stoned.

I puffed it and coughed like crazy.

"Hahaha," they both laughed.

"Strawberry cough," Dave said squinting his eyes, he could barely open them.

"Damn, the kushberries taste like kushberries and the strawberry cough tastes like a strawberry and makes ya cough!!" I exclaimed laughing the smoke out of my lungs and the boys laughed, too, 'til Dave remembered his question.

"Wait sooo, what are we gonna do, bro?" Dave repeated the question.

"I was thinking we could text Travis when we need to, maybe stay here a couple days and camp out, ya know? Deserted island life!" I said.

"No service," Dave said.

"Shihit," Sean said stoned and observing the conversation like he wasn't part of it. He looked like he was at home watching the plot of a movie unfold.

"Well then, worse case scenario, we have to radio for help from the Coast Guard," I said flatly, kind of killing the vibe, even mentioning them.

Sean and Dave winced at the thought knowing we'd probably get in some trouble somehow.

"Yeah, that's what I thought, so let's just enjoy it," I said.

"Yeah, guess you're right," Dave said.

"Yeah, let's chill," Sean said and we all nodded and agreed to just enjoy what could inevitably end with rescue.

"Maybe the phone service will come back as the storm clears over whatever mainland we're near," I said.

"Yeah, it could I guess," Dave said.

"Cheee!" I yelled jumping down off the boat side that was leaning closest to the ground with my spear and fins in hand and goggles on top of my head. "I'm gonna get us some lunch," I said and headed into the water putting my goggles on.

"Woo!" the boys cheered me on.

"I'll get ready to cook it up," Dave shouted.

"I'll roll another blunt!" Sean yelled and I went under.

The water was just as clear maybe somehow clearer as I put my fins on and started swimming around hunting for food. I hovered over colorful reefs of every shape and size covered in little fish with varying patterns and combinations of color staring at me as my dreads entranced them. I was swimming through an expensive fish tank at your favorite restaurant, searching for a big one and not a colorful one, when it revealed its beautifully ugly head around the corner of a big reef in front of me, a hog fish, fat and delicious. It turned back and went the other way soon as it saw me. I jolted right, to go around the reef and cut him off. There we were face to face and the chase was on but I was nearly out of breath. I stayed on his trail of bubbles as he ripped ahead through the water, but I was gaining on him and he knew it. In his last ditch effort he turned to the side to show me how big he really was and I took the shot piercing him straight through the side and pinned him down into the ground to do the kill shot and say a quick word but the spearhead snapped off and got stuck in a coral shelf. Overwhelmed and out of breath I burst out of the shallow water, still holding the spear pinning my kill to the ground.

"Got one!" I yelled panting and trying to catch my breath. "Guys, I got one," I yelled again but I guess they couldn't hear me. I went back down to get it and found myself face to face with a large blacktip reef shark practically snarling at me for this food. I started kicking, swimming frantically backward pushing away from his face, but it kept coming. Its large razor-sharp teeth gnashing at my fins just an inch in front of his face. I loaded the tipless spear I was still holding on my arm and unloaded it into his piercing black eye as I continued to swim backwards using now only legs, that I prayed to God I didn't lose. The shark didn't flinch, and I fired again still nothing as he chased me down unfazed by my broken spear shots. I fired one last time and he turned off probably just to get an easier meal that I had just hunted for him.

I had been going in the right direction and was just about on shore when I saw that horrible familiar sight of flashing lights on my beautiful island and my friends being handcuffed by men in uniform. I ducked back into the water, thinking I might take my chances with the shark. I watched as they stormed our new home I had hardly got to know and enjoy. They were yelling and being aggressive like we had done something really bad. I couldn't let them take the fall for it. I had gotten them into this. I stood up and flip-flopped over to them in my flippers and goggles, but I left the spear.

"Another one!" they yelled and dove on me, throwing me to the ground, breaking my goggles.

"Joey, no!" Dave yelled. "We're gonna sue you for that, dude," he added trying to pull away from the officers holding him back.

"Don't say nothin' boys," I said and they took us away, cuffed and hooded in a helicopter.

They tried us for life in prison adding up all the pounds of weed they discovered and saying we had the intent to distribute, but weed was on the docket to be legalized federally and our lawyers proved we had just found the island not filled it with weed. They let us go and dropped all charges and said sorry for the trouble. I guess we would have had to call them anyways, but who knows.

Me, Sean and Dave met up after the trials were done to burn and reminisce about what happened, but Booger had moved to another state so he wasn't there still. So much time had gone by and lives had changed forever, but somehow sitting there smoking it all felt like yesterday we came up with the plan to adventure.

While we were in jail the news hit the streets that The Seaweed Pirates had been arrested and it created a buzz about us you can't even pay for with all the money in the world. And that one DJ at the radio station kept playing our songs and I guess it spread. We were all over the radio with our three songs we played live there that day. People around the world love our songs and our story so a record label hit us up and paid big money. We hadn't even started spending it yet, we just got out and met up to burn and talk and relax from all that craziness.

"What's good bruddas?" I said greeting them with a fist bump.

"Chilling, chilling," Sean said.

"Yeah, chilling man, we're freaking rich!" Dave shouted and hit the bong in front of him.

"Yeah, what the fuck," Sean said.

"Eye people love The Seaweed Pirates," I said using my pirate voice for the first time since we left the island. We laughed and smoked.

"Wish I knew where that island was still, man, I bet that shit still washes up there," I said taking a hit from a pipe similar to the one from the ship, for memories.

"I dropped a pin," Sean said, "in Dave's phone when we got there," he added.

"You're a fucking genius," I said standing up and shaking him.

"Haha are you serious?" Dave asked pulling out his phone and checking to find that there was in fact a random pin near where Sensemilla Island had been, but there was no land on the map.

"Let's go!" I yelled.

"Haha how?" Dave asked laughing.

"Yes, down!" Sean exclaimed.

"Let's go down and rent a boat, a big boat with big engines though, haha," I laughed and they laughed as we smoked but after that session, that's exactly what we did.

We took a helicopter to the island then rented a boat for the day and went directly to the pinned location. As we pulled up we could see an abandoned boat on the shore. It looked much older of a wreck than ours and was badly broken in many places with big holes in the hull. It looked naked. If that was our boat they had torn it apart and left it to rot. We anchored and went ashore to inspect the boat and hopefully smoke a bunch of weed on the island.

"I'm pretty sure this is it," I yelled running up to the shell of a vessel. It was ripped apart by weather and scavenged by looters, almost unrecognizable, but I could still see on the weathered, rotten, sun-faded stern clearly written was the one word, "FREE."

Printed in Great Britain
by Amazon

58262264R00129